The Job of the Wasp

The Job of the Wasp

A NOVEL

Colin Winnette

Soft Skull  New York

This is a work of fiction. All of the characters, organizations, and events portrayed in this novel are either products of the author's imagination or used fictitiously.

Library of Congress Cataloging-in-Publication Data
Names: Winnette, Colin, author.
Title: The job of the wasp : a novel / Colin Winnette.
Description: First Soft Skull edition. | New York : Soft Skull, 2018.
Identifiers: LCCN 2017038215 | ISBN 9781593766801 (pbk. : alk.
    paper)
Classification: LCC PS3623.I66345 J63 2018 | DDC 813/.6—dc23
LC record available at https://lccn.loc.gov/2017038215

Published by Soft Skull Press
1140 Broadway, Suite 704
New York, NY 10001
www.softskull.com

Soft Skull titles are distributed to the trade by
Publishers Group West
Phone: 866-400-5351

Printed in the United States of America

10 9 8 7 6 5 4 3 2 1

for Ashley

I am—yet what I am none cares or knows.

—JOHN CLARE

The Chapters in This Novel

The Job of the Wasp

ONE IN, ONE OUT

Upon my arrival at the facility, I was asked what I hoped to get out of my time there and how I planned to make myself useful. The sign out front described the building as a school for orphaned boys, so I said my hope was to get a good education, three square meals a day, a place to lay my head, and, in return, I was happy to help out in any way I could.

"This is not a school," said the Headmaster, whose nose was like a mushroom, somehow both silly and threatening. "It is a temporary holding facility with mandatory educational elements. You will be held until you are far enough along to care for yourself. No longer, no less. You will work, along with the other boys, to earn your room and board. You will be provided for, but you will not be comforted. Even if I wanted to comfort you, we have been forced by the economic realities of our situation to live simply. Add to that the fact that, by taking you on, we are now at a whopping thirty-one students, one beyond our maximum capacity as stated in the materials I've presented to the state every semester for more than ten years running. And yet here we are, facing what will likely prove to be one of our most difficult terms in all respects, I am sure of it. Run a facility as long as I have, and you start to develop a nose for these things." He pulled a sheet of paper from his desk drawer and tore it in half. "Regardless, we will clothe you, feed you, and provide you a bed. You'll receive a standard education. Nothing fancy. Enough to get by within these doors. But as far as things go out there"—he pointed toward the heavy oaken doors that had been barred behind me when I walked in—"as far as that goes, you will be on your own."

He pulled a pen from a jar at his right and set to drawing something on the bottom half of the torn paper.

"You'll have various duties," he said. "You'll like some of them and you won't like others. You'll do all of them equally well, because if you stop, or start doing the job carelessly, we will find something else to do with you. And every time we have to reassign you, you will like your new job less—that I can promise you. So do your first job well and you will be as happy as you can possibly be. Do you understand everything I've told you so far?"

"Yes," I said.

"Good," he said. He rose. "It's possible you'll like it here. It's also possible you'll hate it. We're not in the business of guarding memories, only of keeping you from sliding into a lesser existence. You'll have everything you need and a few things more. You will get by. What do you say; will that suffice?"

"Yes," I told him.

"Have you always been so agreeable?" he said.

"I'm sure I haven't," I said. "But I know when it's time to

fight and when it's time to say 'Thank you' and 'I understand' and 'Yes.'"

He eyed me for a moment, then waved me on. It was my belief that our first meeting went well.

At dinner, we were served pork and spinach. It was simple but sat well together on the plate and had a pleasant smell. I nodded as another boy told me that the pork was so tender because the pigs were fattened on the flesh of new boys who could not fit in. His speech was practiced. He had heard it from someone before him, or he had given it many times. He was handsome, I decided. He had little else to say that wasn't about the book he was carrying with him. I hadn't read it, or any of the books he compared it to, because I have no taste for fiction, so I found it harder and harder to listen to him.

"I'd like to focus on my tender pork, if you don't mind," I said.

The boys around us flinched. They seemed to hiss through their teeth.

"You should focus on having a shower," said the bookish boy.

I was in damp and muddy clothes, it was true, and my trouser leg was torn. But I'd been instructed to report directly to the dining hall where dinner was being served and so hadn't been able to tidy up or bathe.

"Did you know," I told the boy, "that we are now one person beyond capacity? The Headmaster instructed me to report back if I had any thoughts on who we might be able to send packing. Anyone who might fare better on the streets than in a civilized facility. There are only so many beds, and there is only so much you can teach a person."

"You are a liar," said the other boy, "and a faggot."

I accepted what he had to say, and he added nothing more.

We were not given salt, only a fork and a napkin. When I was given the fork and the napkin, I was instructed not to lose them. The napkin, I was told, was to keep my uniform clean of pork and spinach once it had arrived. Outside of their providing the napkin, any spills or stains were mine to deal with, and stained uniforms were unacceptable. My measurements would be taken in the morning and I would receive a uniform within a week. Most of the other boys did look sharp. I was looking forward to the uniform, and to blending in.

An aging wooden frame draped in ivy, or some reaching plant like ivy, arched over a brick path that led us from the dining hall after dinner. The ivy held small buds that would blossom in spring, I guessed. I didn't know much about plants, their names or behaviors, but I still enjoyed them.

We had half an hour for recess, and we were to spend it on a rectangle of muddy yard that sat behind the dormitory. A row of saplings articulated the border of our scrappy plot, and at the far end sat a faded blue gazebo.

I inspected the ivy and its buds on the trellis while the other boys played a running game in the dirt. Something put a boy on the sidelines and something else would draw him back in. I was unfamiliar with the rules and was not invited to play, but I did not feel excluded. The game had fallen habitually into place, as a matter of course, and I wasn't yet part of their world.

After recess, we were instructed to study in our rooms. Mine was small but serviceable. It featured a window, a dresser, and a desk. A small bed. A lamp with a green glass shade. I felt like a young professional. A young man setting out to make something of himself in the world. I felt suddenly heartened and hopeful. There was a stack of paper in the desk drawer, along with two pencils. I'd been given nothing to study yet, so I drew pictures. Everything that came to me was violent or bloody. I drew ghosts and soldiers and some things I did not know. I tore up the pages when I was done and put them in a waste bin by the bed.

Before lights-out, the boys all stood in the hall and sang a song together. I did not know the words. Those I could decipher had little meaning to me. From what I could tell, it was a song about loyalty and pride. I thought about this and realized that at that point in my life I was loyal to no one and felt pride for nothing. It was something I hoped to change.

I did not sleep well that first night. In the dark, the room felt like a grave. I heard laughter from outside the window, but only for a moment. I looked and saw nothing out of the ordinary. For the rest of the night, I sat up, waiting for it to happen again.

In the morning, I was called to the Headmaster's office. A small man in suspenders and a striped white shirt was there, and I was made to stand on a stool. He brought up my arms and spread my legs. He gripped each and every part of me, grumbling to himself. The Headmaster was at his desk, drawing on two halves of a torn sheet of paper. When he was finished, he placed one half in a drawer by his right knee and crumpled the other half in his left hand. He held the crumpled paper in a fist, which he gently pulsed as he watched the small man grip me.

"You're fatter than boys your height should be," said the small man.

"I'm sorry," I said.

"I thought you were an orphan," he said. He stepped away from me, inspected my feet, then stepped back in to grip some more.

"Do you have what you need?" said the Headmaster.

"The pants will have to be large in the waist, so they will look baggy around the legs," said the small man. "There's nothing I can do about it. I have too much to do to take on customized work for every fattened orphan sent your way."

"I don't mind if they're baggy around the legs," I said.

"Depending on how baggy they are," said the Headmaster, "it will be fine."

"I don't know how baggy they will be just yet," said the small man. He had drawn a notepad from his back pocket and was sketching something.

"I don't mind if they're baggy," I said again. I brought down my arms.

The small man stepped forward and raised my arms once more.

"If they're too baggy," said the Headmaster, still pulsing the crumpled paper, "we will send them back."

"You have to understand that they are going to be baggy," said the small man, lowering his notepad. "If you don't understand that, then there's going to be trouble."

"It's okay," I said.

"I understand that the pants will be somewhat baggy," said the Headmaster, "but if they are excessively baggy, we are going to send them back."

"You're not getting it," said the small man. "The boy is fat. He needs a special waist. It's a grown man's waist. He does not have the legs of a grown man. The pants are going to be baggy, and they will be too long. I've never seen an orphan so well fed."

"Send the pants," said the Headmaster. "Send pants that he can wear."

The small man left in a huff, leaving the door ajar.

"He's a pervert," said the Headmaster. "Don't pay him any mind at all."

Before class, I was given a long pencil and a dull blade to keep the tip sharp.

"There is a zero-tolerance policy when it comes to violence, threat, or accidental harm," said the teacher. "If you use the blade for anything other than the pencil, you'll be released from the classroom. You'll spend the day working outside, and you will not like the work."

I nodded.

"Don't look so grave," she said. "Our goal is to keep you safe, not to mete out unwarranted punishment. If you use the blade as intended, your day will go fine."

Only a few minutes into class, the boy behind me poked his

blade into the node between my ear and the back of my skull. I yelled out, swung at him, and I was asked to leave the classroom.

"I was told my day would go fine," I said in the hall, where the teacher had angrily planted me on a low bench.

"I saw what I saw," she said. "We haven't time for a trial."

"It isn't fair," I said. "I didn't start it."

"Did you swing at him?" she said. "Did you intend to hit him?"

I said nothing. I crossed my arms at my chest.

"You'll have a job assigned to you as soon as I've settled the other boys," she said.

I waited on the bench until we were all released for lunch.

At lunch, I sat with a group of boys I did not recognize, and we were served spaghetti. The boy to my left asked if I enjoyed marbles.

"Not the game," he said, "but the toy itself."

"How does the game work?" I said.

"I'm not asking about the game," said the boy. "You don't listen."

The boy who'd stuck me with the blade was in the far corner of the room. I could hear him eating from all the way over there, slurping up spaghetti as it unwound from the nest on his plate.

"What's his name?" I asked the boy with the marbles.

"Whose?"

"The boy in the corner there. The blond." I pointed with my fork, dropping a bit of red sauce on the table.

The boy shrugged and dug a sliver of meatball onto his spoon. "You should be more careful," he said.

"You don't know him?" I said.

The boy shrugged again. "I keep to myself," he said.

When I finally received my uniform, it was an ill fit. The pants were baggy from the knees down, and the legs dragged. The Headmaster, who had delivered the brown paper package to my room himself, watched as I tried them on.

"Every boy is to display his hem," he said, as I tried to cuff the overlong legs. "I apologize for the inconvenience, but I do trust you can manage."

"Is there anything we can do to them?" I said, imagining my heel coming down on the hem at the precise moment my body lurched forward, tearing the pants along the seam and shredding them up to the waist.

"New uniforms are provided once every other year," said the Headmaster. "You can trade yours in early, but it will mean a missed opportunity down the line. The traded-for uniform will have to last even longer than the original, and that is a dangerous game to play. I suggest accepting the pants as they are and focusing on losing some weight in the coming year so that when you are fitted with a fresh pair, they will not be too baggy and the legs will not drag."

Though I could accept them, these were stressful terms to accommodate. I would have to put a great deal of effort into not shredding the pants under a clumsy heel. I practiced, walking a few small circles in my room and wincing whenever the hem found its way under my foot. The overall effect was that I appeared much weaker than I actually was, and seemed to be walking with a limp.

"If we could just talk to the tailor," I said.

"The tailor's time with us has ended," said the Headmaster. "The matter is now yours to deal with on your own."

The ivy on the wooden frame did eventually blossom. The petals of each flower crinkled like a receipt in the sun after only a few days, but they had a strong smell, which was made stronger when I rubbed the fallen petals between two fingers. I plucked six or seven of the flowers and brought them into my room, where I imagined they would fare better. I set them in a dish on the windowsill, and a strange yellow oil ran from them, staining the water. I washed and refreshed the dish three times, but there was always more oil. The water was never clear. Still, the petals stayed purple and scented for days before going brown and sinking to the bottom of the dish.

The other boys were not drawn to me, nor was I drawn to them, but I was comfortable on the edges of most social interactions. I didn't involve myself in gossip or trouble. I didn't participate in casual play or study groups. If I wasn't motivated, I stared at the desk or the window until I felt ready to work. I didn't reward laziness. I didn't look to others to solve my problems for me. I was focused and observant when I could be, and patient when I could not.

I was now acutely aware of the boy who sat behind me in class. When he lifted open his desk, I braced myself. When his chair squawked, I pictured him leaning in. I imagined the prick of the blade against the node between my ear and the back of my head, a pain I could recall with unsettling ease. I prepared myself, every time he shifted, for the inevitable prick, coaching myself to accept it and move past it as quickly as possible. I didn't want to invite any more trouble than was already being delivered upon me. When the blow came, I would not react. I would swallow up the blade with the back of my head, and class would continue uninterrupted.

But later, after lights-out, when he was comfortable in his bed and satisfied with all the cruelties he'd managed to deliver upon the innocent members of his cohort without punishment, I would visit him. I would move fast and hard, and make contact with something vital.

That the boy never bothered me again with his blade did not stop me from harboring violent feelings toward him. If anything, those feelings grew in direct relation to the time I spent thinking about them without acting on them. I understood that it was its own form of torture, not pricking me a second time. He had evolved his cruelty into its subsequent phase, which involved my imagining the wound over and over again without the release of its ever actually being delivered. Although I had done nothing to provoke his animosity, it was clear that ignoring it would only make things worse, and that it would have to be dealt with in kind.

Classes did not break for summer, but there was a transitional period at the end of each semester, and during that time certain liberties could be gained by those in the facility's good graces. At the end of the spring term, before summer officially began, the Headmaster called the boys, one by one, into his office for a review of the year so far. When I was summoned, my plan was to convince him I had lost weight—even though it was obvious I hadn't—and not to leave the room until I was confident the meeting had gone well.

There was plenty of work to be done in the summer, and a great deal of difference between indoor and outdoor work. There was shingling and there was filing. There was mopping the dining hall and there was sweeping under the blossoming ivy. In general, I preferred sweeping—slow, measured work with poetic undertones. Stroke by stroke, you were erasing the passage of time, sentencing each path to a purgatory of cleanliness. Under the ivy, the work of sweeping was an even more meditative and humbling practice. By contrast, other jobs, such as dunking dishes in the washing line or emptying waste bins around the facility, were endless and unrewarding. Dull as mud.

If the Headmaster felt I'd kept up my end of the bargain, that I'd so far been putting my time at the facility to good use and was committed in my efforts toward a better fit of pants, it was possible these positive feelings would influence his decision as to my summer chores. He might also see some sense in assigning outdoor work to a boy who was obviously benefitting from exercise, both mental and physical. I needed to sit up straight in his office. I needed to look him in the eye. I needed to be open, confident without being cocky, and, above all, I needed to be honest with him. People can feel the weight of our lies, even if they don't detect them as such. But honesty adds oxygen to a room.

"How are you finding your time here?" said the Headmaster.

"I'm finding it well," I said, "for the most part."

"Where's the trouble?" he said.

"I haven't been sleeping much," I said. "Because I'm fearful at night."

"Fearful of what?"

"If I knew," I said, "I would have a plan for how to deal with it."

He smiled, but there was something troubling in it, as if I'd somehow put him on guard. So I tried again.

"It's either that I'm scared of everything at night," I explained, "or, underneath my daily habits, I am in a state of constant fear obscured by the action of the day, so that as I lie in bed and the rest of the world grows quiet, that general state of fear moves to the front of my mind at a similar rate, grafting onto one subject after another—what I might be hearing outside my window, why there is no moon visible through the glass when, by my calculations, there should be, what another boy in the facility might someday do to me, what might have happened to me in the past, what might happen to all of us in the future, where this building will be in one thousand years, what was here one thousand years before, whether or not I will live as long as I might like to, if something will abruptly cut things short, or if living too long will bring its own unspeakable horrors—the list is endless, and because no item on the list represents on its own the actual, primary source of my fear, it can't be reasoned away, put down, thought out, or fully dealt with. I can only cycle through the endless possibilities, exhausting each item before moving on to the next."

"You are very interested in understanding things and presenting them as they are," said the Headmaster, still guarded but easing up.

"Yes," I said. "I am very interested in truth."

"Then you must know this only works if you're being honest with me." He tore a sheet of paper into two equal parts, then folded one half down the middle, over and over again, until it was too thick to fold anymore.

"I'm being very honest," I told him. "I'm being as honest as I possibly can be."

"Why don't you try again then?" he said. "What, specifically, are you afraid of? Take a moment, if you need it."

"I can't know because it's not a particular thing," I said, "or I can't know because it's too many things to count. It's the honest truth that both are a possibility, and that all the thinking I've done on the subject has brought me no closer to deciding between the two."

He tried to fold the paper again, but it wouldn't budge. "Maybe it isn't fear that you're feeling," he said, "but anxiety."

"Can you tell me the difference?" I said.

He handed me the second half of his paper and pulled a fresh sheet from his desk.

"Fold it," he said.

"In half?" I said.

He nodded. I folded.

"Keep going," he said, and so I folded until the paper would fold no more, just as he had done.

"Do you feel better?" he said.

I thought for a moment.

"Answer honestly," he said.

"No," I said. "I don't feel better."

"Then perhaps it's not anxiety," he said with a shrug. "It's always worked for me."

He set his fat, folded sheet onto a stout pile of similarly folded sheets at the corner of his desk. That I hadn't noticed them before was testament to the level of focus and determination I'd brought to this important meeting.

"So," he said, "you spend hours and hours each night in a general state of fear about everything." It was said tenderly and without accusation.

We were getting somewhere.

"Not everything," I said. "But many things, yes."

"When I met you," he said, "I saw a bright young boy with a promising future. People said you were overweight, but I had faith in you."

"I've lost two pounds, sir," I said. My first of many lies to the Headmaster.

He had already torn and folded a fresh sheet and was now pulling another from his desk. He rubbed the lobe of his left ear between two fingers before setting to work again on the paper. "Is that true?" he said.

I looked at my lap. There was still a large bump there, but when I leaned back it did appear slightly smaller than it might have in the winter. It was possible I'd lost some fat and gained some muscle. My routines had changed. My life had a new shape; why shouldn't I?

"Are you enjoying the food here?" he said.

I paused. "I haven't had much of an appetite," I said.

The Headmaster smiled, again rubbing the earlobe. "It's not the best, is it?" he said.

I shook my head, pinching the lump in my lap.

"Do you think you deserve the best?" he said. "Do you think a group of orphans living in a home should eat better than those of us who work for a living?"

I shook my head again.

"I don't mean to be harsh," he said, releasing the lobe and taking up a fresh sheet. "Remember, I eat the food here too. But I told you on the day we met that comfort isn't something that comes without effort. It's not something people simply provide for you. It's something you strike out for on your own. Something you make for yourself. Something you identify, come to understand, and then pursue. My job is to look after you until you're capable of finding your own comforts—not to be those comforts. I couldn't be if I wanted to, and I also do not want to. What would happen then? You would grow into our facility like a tree taking root, that's what. But I want you to grow out. Not just up, but out, and to never look back."

I nodded, and I saw in his eyes that he was open to me. No longer guarded. We were somehow on the other side of our difficult moment.

"Wouldn't you like that?" he said.

"I would like to grow up and out," I said. "Without putting on any more weight."

He smiled again. Things were going well.

"So, you can enjoy what's good enough for now?" he said.

"It's far from the worst food I've eaten," I said.

At that, the Headmaster laughed. It was remarkable. I'd set out to accomplish something, and here it was accomplished. I couldn't remember having felt more satisfied than I did in that moment.

"No, I suppose it isn't," he said, wiping his nose and still chuckling. "How about your classes? Everything making sense so far?"

"They're fine," I said. "They're good." I relaxed into my seat.

"Which do you like the most?" he said. "Where do you think you'll shine this semester?"

"I don't know," I said. "I've never thought of it that way. I work hard to excel in all of my subjects."

"Okay," he said. "Where do you struggle most academically?"

Reflexively, I thumbed the node between my ear and the back of my skull. Aware of what I'd done only after I'd done it, I tried to make the gesture seem natural, rubbing my palm along the back of my neck and into my hair.

"Math," I said.

"That's an important one," he said. "No reward in slacking there."

"I apply myself most in areas where I am having the most trouble," I said.

"Good," he said. "That's good. And you're getting along with the other boys?"

I nodded.

"No one is giving you any trouble?"

I shook my head.

"How about the boy who sits behind you?" he said.

I was very still.

"He's not giving you any trouble?"

"Who's that again?" I said.

"The boy who sits behind you in the classroom. He hasn't given you any trouble at any point?" He tore a fresh sheet of paper and began to draw on its bottom half.

I knew I couldn't be honest with the Headmaster about my feelings toward the boy, not without risking everything I'd gained over the course of our meeting. But the teacher had obviously told the Headmaster something, and I would have to address it now if I wanted him to believe I was still being honest with him. It was likely she'd reported what I'd done, and it followed that she would have passed on my explanation for it. If the Headmaster was inviting my side of the story in an effort to balance the scales of justice, it was too late. Were administrative trouble to find its way to the boy at this point, the others would think I'd been the one to follow up with the Headmaster, possibly for the sole purpose of confirming punishment for the other boy involved. This would murder my already miserable reputation and invite a great deal more trouble. Additionally, justice at the hands of the uninvolved simply wouldn't satisfy the days I'd spent living in phase two of the boy's evolved cruelty, wherein, though he'd technically done nothing, things had taken a sinister turn.

The Headmaster looked up from his paper, which he'd pinned to his desk with one hand.

"Well?" he said.

I was trapped. What I'd seen moments before hadn't been comfort or good will, but the patient confidence of a hunter who would successfully lure in his prey. He wanted nothing less than the full story, which he'd known I would be hesitant to give. Now I could only affirm my guilt by yielding to the teacher's account, possibly abandon credibility with a lie, or lose control of the situation by telling him everything, placing my fate in the hands of a boy who would undoubtedly seek retribution for whatever punishments followed. Considering my options, I felt I had no choice but to venture further from the truth.

"The boy poked me once with the end of his pencil sharpener," I said. "While I no longer believe it was on purpose, I lost my temper at the time, sir, and I tried to hit him. I was punished for it on the day."

"How could he have accidentally poked you with the end of his pencil sharpener?" said the Headmaster.

"I don't know," I said. "But I'm convinced he didn't mean to."

"What convinces you?" he said.

"The boy and I get along very well," I said. "We got along before and after he poked me. He's apologized for the accident, and we've put it behind us."

"He did?" said the Headmaster.

I nodded.

"Did he explain how the accident happened?" he said.

"I took him at his word," I said. "Honesty necessitates trust."

"Well, I'm glad to hear things came to such a peaceful conclusion," he said. "If that's all, you're now excused."

Shocked, but pleasantly so, I rose, watching the floor while shoving my folded paper into a trouser pocket. I'd promised myself I would stay until I was positive things had gone well, but now it seemed far better to leave before I somehow made matters worse.

"One last thing," said the Headmaster as I approached the door. "What's his name again?"

"Who's that?" I said.

"The boy who sits behind you," he said. "Remind me of his name?"

I thought a moment. "It never came up," I said.

"Interesting," he said. "Through all those apologies and getting along."

"I assure you it was an accident with a peaceful resolution," I said. "If I misspoke, it's because I was caught off guard by it even being a topic of conversation."

"Okay," he said. "Then I thank you for your time. And for your honesty, of course."

"It didn't even hurt," I told him. "It was more a grazing than a poking, sir."

"That's good to know," he said.

"We're friendly now," I assured him, "but it's only the beginning of the friendship."

"When you join the other boys in the washing line," he said, "try to stick yourself somewhere in the middle without being disruptive. And send in the next boy as you leave."

That night, I thought I heard the laughter again, but I did not get up. A new boy had been seated behind me in class that afternoon. The boy who'd stuck me was gone. But the teacher had done nothing to acknowledge the change, and the other boys didn't seem to register it.

He hadn't been in the dining hall either, nor in the dorms for the nightly song. When no one said anything, I eagerly followed suit. But now the laughter lapped at the edges of my window, and I couldn't help feeling that some great injustice was about to be brought down upon me.

I listened as the laughter moved in and out of audibility. I could smell smoke too, or something like smoke. And there was a voice—indecipherable at first, but soon it rang clear.

"Snitch," it said.

"Rat." That was a second voice coming through the window.

I rose to look through the glass but again saw no one. The yard was empty in all directions. The saplings were bent in the wind. The grass was weak too, bowed over and rippling.

"If someone's out there," I said to the glass, "I'll drown you like a field mouse."

Nothing else happened before the ceiling screamed, and I was showered in cool water. My bed, my clothes, my hair. The papers on my desk slid soaking to the floor where a puddle was already gathering. Boys shrieked in the hall, with equal parts terror and delight. A red light came on then went off then came on then went off. I went to the door and looked out. My vision was obscured by the water pouring down my face, into my eyes, falling from the ceiling and all around us.

A boy slid past on his heels.

"What's happening?" I called.

He shook his head in a falsely sympathetic way. "Sprinklers," he said, pointing up.

Boys filed past me then, headed to the yard to gather: a protocol I'd been left to discover on my own. It was a cold night, and it wasn't long before the wet lot of us started to shiver. Groups of friends gathered together, warming each other vaguely with their proximity. Frightened, angry, I stood alone at the edge of the crowd, looking for anyone in dry clothes. Anyone who might have been outside when the water started to fall.

After some time, the Headmaster appeared at the edge of

the yard in his robe and pajamas. He was dry, but that was an unlikely lead. He wore white slippers that were gathering mud at the edges as he moved toward us.

"Who's done it, then?" said the Headmaster.

No one spoke.

"Every year," said the Headmaster, "some unimaginative little onion pulls that switch and brings you all out here soaked and shivering, as you each are now. Do you know, and I'm speaking to all of you here, how incredibly tired this prank of yours is? If you did, I think you would derive less pleasure from it. I hope it reduces whatever pleasure you might be deriving currently to know that I am not bothered in the slightest to have to get out of bed at this hour in order to address the soaking lot of you, bothered far less than you surely are, cold and wet and shivering like eels on ice. I have a fire burning in my home as I speak. My wife is setting logs on that fire, and it is snapping out into the room, it's so hot and excited for me to join it with a glass of brandy, which I will pour to ease the pity I might still be feeling upon my return. That's right: Pity is what I'll feel. Maybe the faintest bit of irritation, but mostly pity. Pity and disappointment. You might reconsider your situation, soaked and standing in a muddy field. You call this a prank? Here is the result of your effort. Here is your good time. Here is your joke. You, I should say, are your joke. You and the boys who support your very few pleasures in life. The boys who do your laundry and wash your dishes and serve your pork. While we stand out here together and let the night settle into our bones, awaiting the fire department, I want you all to think very carefully about how much fun this actually was. How delightful. What a gas.

THE JOB OF THE WASP

It's a costly prank to the school, to be sure, and one without reward. Funny as you might think it is, the only ones who suffer from this expense are the lot of you. My salary doesn't change. My home is as it will always be. You, however, have just forfeited to the state a large sum of money that could and would have been spent on your education, your meals, the luxuries you are being provided for free, perhaps undeservingly; it's not up to me to decide. It's a waste of everyone's time, these little pranks, these little repetitions, and it rattles young immune systems. Who knows what diseases some of you will wake up with? Who knows how little medicine there is to go around? I was wrong before. Allow me to correct what I said. It's exclusively pity that I feel. Pity and boredom, that is. Year after year and here we are. Such a bother and such a waste."

He trailed off as he waddled from the center of our attention. He closed his robe at the waist and leaned himself against a young tree several feet away from the group.

"Did you see his face?" said one of the boys. "Those pajamas?"

"Classic," said another. "The best one yet."

It was some time before the fire department came. If the building had indeed been burning, there wouldn't have been much left to save. The firefighters looked exactly as I had imagined firefighters would look. They had large hats and yellow jackets. They were carrying axes. There was an enormous Dalmatian sitting on a bed in the back of the truck, and one firefighter approached the animal with water in a silver dish. They had the

Headmaster give a brief statement and sign a form. He made us stand outside and witness all of it. It was not the coldest I've ever been, but it was still remarkably cold.

The firefighters had arrived with sirens blaring, but they left with little fanfare. Just the brake lights burning and a few of the boys hollering after them to honk the horn once more. They didn't.

We filed back to our waterlogged quarters, and the Headmaster left for his home just down the hill. Some of the boys were still laughing. One was wiping his eyes while his friend with similar hair tried to entertain him, striking fierce poses like a dancer or a street performer. The mass of them moved down the hall like foam.

I was a silent observer, trying not to be noticed or interacted with. Not one of these boys was to be trusted. They'd spent too many years on their own, too many years viewing themselves as separate from the rest of the world—separate but as a unit. One or several of these boys had pulled that alarm. One or several of these boys, perhaps the same one or several, or an entirely different one or several, had been outside my window, laughing and smoking and whispering to me just a moment before the water was released.

I recalled then my threat to drown them. How soon after the water fell. I ground my nails into my palms, watching their faces and looking for signs of guilt. Who was watching me? Who was *not* watching me? I looked for anything at all, keeping to myself and trying to go unnoticed, until I was pushed from behind and fell face-first into the water.

My chin struck the floor and the pain flared up, causing my eyes to water, tears to come pouring down my face. When my hands went to my jaw, something wet worked its way down my wrists, into the sleeves of my nightshirt. Boys filed past. None of them stopped. I would have felt invisible except that the group parted down the middle to move around me, and one or two boys pointed.

"He's soaked," they said.

You will die by my hand, I thought, though I was surprised to realize I felt that way, and a little frightened by it.

I was startled then by a boy I didn't know, who slid his hands into my armpits and helped me up. It was awkward and painful. My body was not ready to be lifted. I was not used to being touched, in general.

"What are you doing?" I said.

"You looked like you needed help," he said.

"It's not bad," I said, putting my hand to my chin again. "It doesn't hurt at all."

"I think that means it was a bad fall," he said.

"I was pushed," I said.

"By whom?" he said.

"If I knew, I would be dealing with it," I said.

"How would you deal with it?" he said, grinning now.

"That's between me and the dead men," I said, confident that anyone who could find something in my suffering to grin at was worthy of suspicion.

"Very strong words," he said.

"Words and deeds," I said.

"You know," he said, "people don't like you."

"What's that?" I said.

"Most people here," he said, "don't like you. You've made enemies."

"Then so have they," I said. "Or one, anyway."

"Right," he said.

"Are you an enemy?" I said, ready with a fist in each hand. It had been a long night.

"No," he said. "I never liked Fry."

"Who is Fry?" I said.

"He used to sit behind you," he said. "Before you showed up, he would hold my face to the shoe pile."

On wet days, we piled our shoes on a mat outside the dining hall. You could smell it through the windows, and it was a bleak bog where reptiles went to expire.

"I didn't do anything to Fry," I said.

"And yet he's gone," said the boy.

"I don't know anything about that," I said.

"Right," he said. "I'll leave it between the two of you, then."

"I'd like to make an appeal to the group," I said. "I had nothing to do with whatever's happened to Fry, and I'd like everyone to know."

"I'm not going to claim you didn't do the right thing," he said, grinning from ear to ear. "You've saved yourself a lot of trouble, as Fry was only getting started with you. But just because I understand you doesn't mean the others ever will."

"It isn't fair," I said. "I haven't done anything."

"Fair or not," he said, still grinning, "you've cast your lot."

There was still water on the floor of my room in the morning. It came to just above my small toe, so I took my clothes from the dresser and dressed on my bed, where it was dry. I cuffed the pant legs, against instruction, and carried my shoes and socks into the hall. There was water there too, running the length of the corridor and into each boy's room.

The others were coming out of their rooms, splashing water with the edges of their feet or trying to figure out some way to dress without getting their socks and pants wet. One boy slid by on his belly, sending a spray through the open doors on either side of him. He made a high-pitched whooping sound as he went, like a war cry.

The floor of the bathroom was also a puddle. I touched my chin and it still felt wet, so I grabbed a handful of toilet paper from the dispenser and carried it, along with my shoes, to the far end of the hall and out the door.

Water rushed down the steps as I stepped out and over to a narrow stone path that led around the building to the yard. I walked barefoot along the cool stones until I reached the old gazebo. It was pale blue on the outside and decorated on the inside with cobwebs, wasps' nests, desiccated moths, and a pulsing cluster of daddy longlegs. Overall, an improvement on the hall of unbridled children. I folded the toilet paper and held it to my chin until it stuck. The structural supports of the gazebo were weathered. The bricks that held its base were soft and crumbling, like chalk. I finished dressing and laced my shoes, watching the other boys pour damply from the hall. Still no Fry. Which meant there were now thirty of us altogether. Capacity, on the nose.

At breakfast, I spotted the boy who'd helped me up the night before. He was at a table of six, three boys to each short bench. There might have been room for me if one or two of them were willing to scoot over, but not a single boy moved in either direction as I approached. The one who'd helped me the night before did not look up.

I ate alone at a table full of boys I had not yet interacted with. I sat across from a skinny one who was having trouble keeping his glasses on his face. He pushed them up the bridge of his nose until they pressed into his brow, and when he drew his hand away they again sank slowly back down to the bulges of his nostrils.

"Set them on your tray," I said.

"I can't see without them on my face," he said.

"What's there to see?" I said. "You've seen this room enough to last a lifetime, haven't you?"

"Why are you picking on me?" he said.

"I'm not," I said. "I'm trying to help."

"Worry about yourself," he said.

The toilet paper on my chin was now crisp and dry. "It's there to cover the wound," I said, touching it.

His glasses slid again, this time failing to catch at his nostrils and finishing the job instead by sliding off and directly into the small square of his tray committed to beef stew.

I took no pleasure in seeing him suffer. Or I took no pleasure in seeing him suffer until I realized I knew his face. Now that I was seeing it in full, now that I could focus on his face as it was, and not as it was when struggling with the glasses, I recognized him as the boy who sat in the row behind me in class, very near to where Fry used to sit. Close enough to have possibly inspired his loyalty to Fry, if only to keep out of the devilish boy's crosshairs.

"You sit behind me in class," I said.

"That was Fry," he said.

"But you sit by Fry," I said.

"I sat by Fry," he said.

"And you two are friends," I said.

"We were friends," he said.

"Where's he gone to then?" I said. "What's become of him?"

"Like you don't know what happened to Fry," he said.

"Why would I know what happened to Fry?" I said.

"Right," he said. "Why would you know."

I had no appetite. I dumped my tray without saying anything more to the boy with soiled glasses, making note of his face as I left. In my head, I drew a picture. If he'd once joined forces with Fry simply to avoid Fry's wrath, he was a weasel. He might not have been bloodthirsty enough to push me from behind in the hall, but he still wasn't to be trusted. He might have been a voice outside my window. He might have pulled the alarm. Who knew where his loyalties, however ill-founded, would lead him, or what he was willing to do to save his own skin?

I spent recess on the edge of the yard, watching the other boys chase one another and slap each other in the testicles. Civilized boys are barbaric in their play, and, to me, every single one of them seemed murderous.

The laundry was done once a week, so I still had the fully folded paper from the Headmaster in my pocket. I stood there feeling equally murderous, waiting for the next step, thumbing the folded paper in my pocket for several minutes, before

COLIN WINNETTE

finally sliding it out and unfolding it with the intention of folding it up again to see if that would calm me down.

If there's something you'd like to confess, it read, *any time is a good time to do so.*

I hadn't noticed the message before, or it hadn't been there. Both were possible, but neither seemed to matter now. If I was meant to confess in the Headmaster's office, I'd failed, and if I was meant to confess now, in the middle of recess, I had no idea to whom I was to offer the confession. And what was there to confess? Fry and I might have harbored violent feelings for one another, albeit for different reasons, but he was the only one so far who'd acted on them. The only question that remained was: How many times could I cross the Headmaster before he turned resolutely against me? Or was it already too late?

I folded the paper along the exact same lines as before, but my mood did not improve. I dug a small hole in the dirt of the yard with my toe and placed the folded paper there, smothering it with my heel.

The other boys were pulling each other's pants down and spitting into one another's hair. All of them were screaming.

Any fears I'd held of having upset the Headmaster were assuaged when, after recess, I was put on garden duty.

The assignment, as unpleasant as it could be, was still one of the more preferable jobs, and it was celebrated as such. Receiving it clearly indicated that, though my standing with the other boys was worse than ever, the Headmaster remained on my side. His note might not have been an appeal to my conscience at all, but a private message between co-conspirators.

32

It's you and me versus the animals, it might well have said. *Consider me a port in the approaching storm.*

The garden was nearly a quarter mile from the facility's main building, a little less than halfway between our dormitory and the Headmaster's home. It had once been used as part of the curriculum, or so I was told, but now the rows of tomato plants and lettuce were choked with weeds. Lumpy squash rotted on the vine. What was left of garden duty consisted mainly of dealing with the waste and decay. We were to weed what we could and collect the rotten fruit and vegetables for dumping elsewhere. Supposedly, when the garden was part of the curriculum, the boys feasted on the products of their labor at least once a week during high season. But now, at best, the plants yielded a handful of edible sundries, most of which hosted burrowing insects, worms and wasps and the like, revealed to us only if we were excited enough by the sight of something edible to transport it back to the kitchen and split it open.

The other boy assigned to the garden was silent for most of the walk. I didn't know him and was happy to keep my distance, provided he kept his. I carried the long tools, two rakes and a hoe, and had a trowel shoved into each pocket. He pushed a wheelbarrow full of fresh dirt. We were to weed, dump the dirt, and use the wheelbarrow to carry away the rotten produce. I imagined our skin would burn some in the sun.

"If we're going to spend the afternoon together, you could at least say something every now and then," he said as the garden came into view.

"I don't have anything to say just yet," I said.

"It's polite to come up with something," he said, "when faced with a length of time alone with a stranger."

"Thank you then," I said, "for taking that first step toward making this less awkward between us."

A few moments later, we'd arrived at the garden. I set the long tools and the trowels at its edge.

"If you weed," I said, "I'll collect the rotten fruit."

This wasn't agreeable to him, and he requested we play a quick hand game to settle the issue of our individual responsibilities. I didn't know the rules, so he explained them to me.

"Knuckles," he said, "is about not being a pansy."

"Okay," I said.

"I'll hold my knuckles out," he said, "and you hit them with your knuckles. Then we'll switch. We go back and forth like that until one of us admits he's a pansy and quits."

"Okay," I said.

"You have to actually say the words," he said, "for the game to end."

"One of us does," I said.

He held out two fists, knuckles up. There was a blackbird holding in the air far above us. I could smell the garden on the wind.

"I just bring my knuckles down onto yours?" I said.

"Hard as you can," he said. "And I will do the same."

I raised my fists and brought them down with as much force as I could manage. The garden dirt was soft, so I was clumsy in my footing. Our knuckles popped, and the pain of it was like five little picks piercing the joint of each finger. The other boy shook out his hands, sucking through his teeth. Then he made two fists, once again.

I might have hit harder if we were on solid ground, I realized, but that was for my next turn. I made two fists, as he had, and already it hurt to bend my knuckles. He had set me up by allowing me to go first. The pain I would feel upon receiving my first blow would be enhanced by the blow I'd just delivered. Every step of the way, I would be one blow ahead. I saw the game unfolding over the next few minutes. Our knuckles splitting, one by one. A curve of dull bone showing through skin.

The other boy was smiling, pleased at having tricked me. I let my wrists hang.

"I'm a pansy," I said.

"Absolutely," he said, opening his fists and examining his knuckles. "I'll weed then," he said, "and you can gather up the garbage fruit."

He called me Pansy as we worked.

"Pumpkin here, Pansy," he said. "Or something like it."

"Rabbit, Pansy," he said. "Two days dead."

I've never cared what people call me. I piled the rabbit on the pumpkin in the wheelbarrow. It was like a poem. Nicknames are like poems in that they are two of the least important things in the world. What use is there in talking about something in the language of what it is not?

There was a fingerling potato sticking up out of the dirt, pink and clean. I gripped it with a fist and pulled hard to dislodge it from its roots. Not only did the potato hold its ground, but the unresolved force of my yank nearly toppled me. The potato was sticking out a little higher than before, but only slightly. I moved closer, trowel in hand. It wasn't until I bent over to dig the thing out that I noticed part of it was coated with what looked like a shell. A pink surface with a little white sliver at its tip and a faint echo of that sliver down at the base, where the flesh of the pink potato began. I dug at the edges of the potato until it revealed itself.

PORNOGRAPHY

I had seen several naked body parts belonging to a woman, but never a completely naked female body, until that sore-knuckled afternoon in the facility garden. She was only a few inches under the dirt, our teacher, whose name I should really have taken the time to learn, I realized, as we were wiping the mud from her eyes.

The other boy kept saying "Oh no," as if I needed to be reminded of how unpleasant it all was.

I used the trowel to dig down and around the corpse, which wasn't even stiff yet. She was heavy, but we could have easily lifted her out of the mud if the other boy had helped me.

Instead, he said, "Oh no."

"How did she get here?" I said.

"We have to hide her," he said.

"I don't follow," I said.

"Someone put her here," he said, "so that no one would find her. We've found her. I don't want to find out what happens next."

"You think she was murdered?" I said.

"Look at her face," he said.

There were no wounds on the body that I could see, but it was true her expression was one of abject horror. The lower jaw seemed unhinged. Her fingers were spread open and curled back, as if she would be forever defending herself against her attacker.

The other boy was right to observe that someone must have put her here, but it was a suspiciously unsuitable place for a corpse anyone truly wanted to store beyond the possibility of casual discovery. It occurred to me then that this might have been the very reason we had been rewarded with garden duty so early in the season. The goal hadn't been to keep someone from finding the corpse, but to bury it so that it might be discovered without any trouble at all.

The Headmaster's note—*If there's something you'd like to confess, any time is a good time to do so*—took on a potential meaning I had not yet considered. I had assumed his thinking was guided by at least an undercurrent of sympathetic rationality, meaning the note was a kind gesture made in the spirit of trust and reconciliation. *I see you have something to say, and I want you to know it's okay to say it.* But if the Headmaster was in fact mad, by which I mean if his thinking was governed by a violently subjective *irrationality*, then it stood to reason that, in our second meeting—which had possibly gone well, in spite of how I'd felt toward the end—he might have grown suspicious, or even become convinced, that the teacher had lied to him about what transpired between me and Fry. I'd insisted on one thing, she on another, and if the Headmaster had believed me—a new boy in a bad situation—over a woman he'd once trusted enough to appoint as an extension of the facility's authority, of his own authority, it was undoubtedly because she had been caught lying before. While it was hard to believe that a single lie could have resulted in her murder, it was not so hard to imagine that a series of lies on her part could have added to a pressure already existent within him, against which he'd battled all his life, making this final lie, however minor, enough to push a long-struggling man over the edge. What was all that folding, if not something to keep his otherwise potentially murderous hands occupied? The note, I now understood, could have come from a part of him that sensed he was on the brink of something grave and irreversible, meaning it had been nothing short of a desperate plea for me to save this woman's life. If I had revealed myself to him in that moment as the source of our discrepancy, I could have been punished more reasonably, as I was a first-time offender and hadn't yet established a habit of lying. I was new to the facility and maybe a little afraid. A first lie, a single lie, only meant I hadn't yet realized I was safe and that he could be trusted. But a pattern of lies, a history of lies, compulsive dishonesty, undermined the structural integrity of any relationship—professional, personal, or otherwise. And perhaps, in the case of the teacher, the Headmaster was finished with being undone.

Her nudity suggested it was a crime of passion. Something personal had been shared between her and her murderer, moments before the final act. Perhaps her lies had wounded him so deeply precisely because their relationship exceeded its professional capacity. I couldn't stop myself from imagining the Headmaster bent backward over the teacher's desk. A mud-covered breast in each hand. Her gnarled fingers guided through his silver hair.

"It's horrific," said the other boy. "Cover it up."

"I don't think this is something we can easily or success-fully keep a secret," I said.

"I say we fill in the dirt and finish our work," he said, "and never talk about this again."

Above us, clouds were gathering. The blackbird was gone. The body had no smell. I imagined for a moment that it was still alive. That she would sit up, maybe ashamed or maybe proud, and cover herself with one of the larger leaves from the pumpkin's vine.

"We'll play knuckles to decide how we handle it," I said. "If I win, we'll alert the authorities immediately, come what may. If you win, we'll cover her up and take the secret to our grave."

I stared at him.

"You already lost once," he said.

"That was different," I said. "This is for this."

"You'll go first then," he said, "because loser goes first."

I nodded. He curled his fingers and made two fists. He held out his arms. I made two little fists as well and brought one squarely to his jaw.

I hadn't meant to hurt him all that badly, only to take control of the situation. But the ground was soft and it was easy to lose your balance, as I've said. He was sent back and over by the punch, almost like the long board of a seesaw. And suddenly he was in the dirt.

They were like two vegetables in a row, the corpses, and it was starting to rain. The boy's left leg was twitching, but it was clear he was done for. The twitch was only nerves. I'd heard we do that. It's one way in which we're like insects, I'd been told.

The staff of the garden hoe extended from behind the boy's head like a diagram. His skull must have been made of paper, the poor thing.

I didn't wait for any more rain to fall and offered his body no comforts or condolences. Instead, I ran in the direction of the facility's main building, where the Headmaster was surely still in his office and a phone could be used to call the paramedics, the morticians, the landscapers, whoever helped in situations like these. Whoever could clear and clean all of this up. I was upset, but with my distress came a level of relative clarity. The work ahead of me was known, and the steps to begin it were well within my reach.

It was a tragedy, no doubt, what had been done to the teacher and what had happened to the boy, but there were upsides to that tragedy, which I could see even while in the midst of it. There were long-term, as well as immediate, benefits to be gained. If the Headmaster had in fact murdered the teacher and buried her in the garden, all the better that I was now a murderer as well. I wasn't proud of the accident, but I knew it granted me exclusive grounds on which to approach the Headmaster in a more direct and intimate way. I could be trusted. I wasn't one to judge.

The rest of the boys were still working at their chores. Some were on the dish line. I could see others through the building's large windows, picking at the trellises of its façade. I slowed to walk calmly past them all. It was really too late to rush, and there was no reason to cause the innocent undue distress.

The Headmaster was in his office, examining a sheet of paper. He must have had a near-endless supply in his lower desk drawers. I was sure he refreshed them on a schedule, every week or even every morning, with obsessive regularity. How fragile his grip on the world must be, I decided, and how severe the consequences for those who interrupted his compulsions.

"That was fast," he said, setting down the page.

"There is a situation," I said.

"I'm aware," he said, "which is why I sent Hannan to fetch you."

"Hannan?" I said.

"Yes, Hannan," he said. "You can be sure Greta would be deeply disturbed if she were to find out."

"Who?" I said.

"Ms. Klein," he said.

That was her name. Ms. Klein. I could hear the other boys chanting it now. *Great Greta Klein. Great Greta Klein. What will it take for me to make her mine?*

"To where did you send Hannan?" I said.

"To the garden," he said, "to fetch the boy responsible for this."

The Headmaster lifted the sheet he'd been examining. It was a drawing of a naked woman, finely shaded. She was leaned against the white of the page in a vulgar position.

"Just now?" I said.

"What are we going to do about this?" he said.

Beneath his concerned expression, I could detect the faintest bit of levity. A grin that had not quite made it to his mouth.

I'd been wrong about the Headmaster, I realized, almost entirely.

This drawing, and his self-satisfaction at the timing of its presentation, was evidence enough that he'd never been on my side, never been seeking to curb his impulses, but had instead delighted in staging an elaborate framing of his newest student. This drawing, which he obviously hoped to pin on me, was clearly of his own creation. He'd murdered Ms. Klein, stripped her of her clothes, buried her where I would be forced to discover her, and was now planting evidence of an illicit relationship, real or imagined, obsessive either way, that I might have been carrying on with her. Hannan, if he'd even ever sent Hannan down, had likely seen me push the other boy and then sit with the two corpses for some time, drawing up my plan of action while coping with the shock of it all. From a distance, that shock might have appeared menacing, even celebratory. I can't be asked to know how someone might misread a desperate scene like that. And now the Headmaster was hiding Hannan somewhere, surely under the auspices of protecting him from the facility's murderous new arrival.

My supposed guardian sat before me, a man in no rush. I could feel in the patience he exhibited while I sorted this all out that I was on the right track. Though his plan had not yet revealed itself to me in full, I could see its outline, feel its shape, and I needed only to fill in the details. Why couldn't he have disposed of the body in the lake? Or ground it up and fed it to the pigs I'd been hearing so much about? Why plant it right under our noses then send us off to sniff around? Why bother framing anyone at all?

He set the drawing face-down on the desk.

"If you're going to claim you didn't do it," he said, "then I would ask you how it wound up in your room."

"Someone planted it," I said, hoping that by hinting at my understanding of what he was up to so far, I might provoke him to slip in some way and definitively confirm my suspicions.

He reached behind him to a low shelf and produced a pile of pages. I could see the geometries of a naked body through the back of each page as he thumbed slowly through them.

"There are sketches here," he said. "Bits and . . . pieces. Add to them the finished work found under your mattress. A substantial time investment, and a fairly elaborate staging, if indeed that is what you are proposing. More likely, these are the products of a young pervert who's been working away at his unsavory project for a while now."

I couldn't describe what I felt then as a release, but a great deal of tension did vanish from my body. The sheer excess of drawings was key to understanding why this all did not begin and end with the disposal of a single body. Yes, the Headmaster was the creator of these drawings, and their existence firmly established the inappropriate relationship I'd originally only supposed. Here was proof of the intimate time the Headmaster had spent with our teacher. The study he'd made of her. There were likely troves of evidence to this illicit relationship, scraps scattered around the facility, which these two had carelessly allowed to accumulate during their oblivious carnival of passion. More than to just get rid of the body, the Headmaster needed a story that would explain or discredit any evidence that might turn up, not only of her murder but of his perverse idolization of her and their subsequent tawdry trysts.

He slapped the pile of pages to his desk, sighing theatrically, so prepared was he to put his plan into action and reinforce the roles he'd written for us. I could see there was no longer any upside to a direct approach, and that I would be forced to wage war on a field of his design.

"I ask again," he said. "What are we going to do about this?"

"I have to accept full responsibility," I said.

"That's a start," he said.

"I don't know what came over me," I said. "I haven't been able to stop thinking about Great Greta Klein since I arrived."

He grimaced.

"I haven't been able to take control of my hand," I said. "When I'm alone in my room, it's all I think about. There is something wrong with me."

"It's not an appropriate practice," he said. "But it's understandable. You are a young boy in a facility full of young boys. She is the only woman in your life. If it weren't for my beautiful wife . . ." He stopped there. I might have heard a tremble in his voice.

"Thank you," I said, "for understanding. But we both know it was wrong of me. Imagine if our poor teacher had discovered these drawings? Imagine if I had kept on drawing them until the room overflowed with them and they spilled out into the hall, into the classroom, into the libraries of our great state?"

He nodded.

"So you're going to stop?" he said.

"Of course," I said. "Do you think I could bear to face this kind of humiliation more than once in my lifetime? I'm mortified by your discovery. I feel my darkest secret has been unearthed, exposed to the scrutiny of strangers and God himself."

I watched his face.

"These days, ours is a secular facility," he said.

I wondered then how old the Headmaster was. It was impossible to tell from his face, where he seemed to carry more years than one life could account for. The only thing I knew for certain was that he'd passed beyond the stage of *aging* and was well into that of *aged*.

"I accept full responsibility, and I ask that you commandeer all of my drawing materials until further notice," I said. "Until this demon has been privately exorcised from my wrist. I beg you."

"Well, try to keep yourself calm," he said. "I don't mean to punish you for having impulses you don't yet know what to do with. Out of respect for Ms. Klein and this facility, though, this practice has to stop. And I agree with you: I should collect your drawing materials and keep them until further notice."

"Excellent," I said. "I'll return to the garden, then, to complete my weeding, and will bring you the materials before dinner."

"It's already getting late," he said. "You can finish your work tomorrow."

"Sir," I said. "This is something I must do. I need to feel the weight of my mistakes. I need to blister."

"First," he said, settling into his chair, "you should be wearing gloves when you're working out there. Second, the sun is going to set momentarily. And third, it's raining. Your garden duty is over for the day."

It was true. The rain had not let up. It had only grown more severe.

"I should at least go gather up the tools," I said. "They'll ruin."

He nodded, and I saw in that simple gesture all that he knew and did not know. If Hannan had already returned with his report, there was no way the Headmaster would have allowed me to return to the scene. That I'd already unearthed Ms. Klein, the fate of the boy in the garden—the Headmaster would never have let me out of his sight if he knew these things. In what he did not know, there was hope for me yet.

"Gather up the tools," he said, "alert your partner, and be done with it all. After that, you can clean up and go to your room. Gather any other pictures you might have squirreled away and bring them to me to be destroyed with the rest."

I ran back to the garden. There was no sign of Hannan along the way. The hill leading down to the garden was slick with rain, and as soon as the bodies came into view, I lost my footing, sliding forward on my rear for several feet before finally catching myself with both hands. I stood again and checked for wounds. I was covered in mud, but already the rain was washing it away.

The water had worn down the edges of the hole that held Ms. Klein. It was collecting around her too, but she was not yet submerged. She seemed almost a part of the earth, like a stone relief, a naked body worn into obsidian. I could see the veins in her breasts like serpents under the surface of the ocean. I set my hands to her, and she was cold and rubbery. She was heavy, but I could move her. I lifted her, her top half and then the lower, into the wheelbarrow. It wanted to topple at first, but I dug its legs into the mud and somehow managed to keep it upright.

Then there was the other boy, whose name I still did not know. There was a great deal of blood at the back of his head, and more when I removed the garden hoe. He was lighter than the teacher, but it was much more difficult to move him.

Piled in the wheelbarrow together, I could inch them wherever I pleased, but I would not describe the overall task as easy. The blood on my hands and wrists ran the lengths of my arms, absorbing into the sleeves of my shirt. It was several hundred yards to the lake, and the mud made it slow work.

I'd never visited our lake before and was surprised to find a small boathouse at its edge, infested with wasps, as all our buildings seemed to be. They were huddled in their nests when I arrived, ignoring me as I steered the wheelbarrow onto the dock's wooden planks. The laden wheel clicked at the gaps between the boards until I was near the dock's far edge, where a canoe had been tied to one of the posts. I untied the rope from the canoe, letting the narrow craft drift toward the middle of the lake, where it stalled, jerking and tipping in the rain.

Getting the corpses out of the wheelbarrow was easier than getting them in. I tied one end of the rope around them, binding them together. I tied the other end to a rock I found at the edge of the boathouse, near a low, metal pipe that was sticking up out of the ground and filling with water. I left Ms. Klein and the boy where they were, then carried the rock to the water and dropped it in. The rope tugged the corpses an inch or so along the dock before the rock settled at the bottom of the lake. I crouched behind the bodies and pushed them over the edge.

They hit the lake with a slap and bobbed in the water until the boy rose up like a pale buoy, holding Ms. Klein just under the surface. The rain rinsed his face, the wasps pulsed in their nests, and I climbed into the lake to finish it.

Waist deep, I gripped the rope and tried to throw the rock into deeper water, but it sank the moment it left my hand, drawing the corpses down by an inch or so, before they re-emerged in the same arrangement as before. I took the rope in hand, dragging the anchor until it was too deep for me to stand and I let the rock start pulling me down.

I swam toward the center of the lake, drifting deeper and deeper, until my lungs grew tight and I had to go up for air. I kicked out from under where I imagined the corpses would be and swam toward the lake's surface, which the rain was working like a sewing machine. I treaded water there, catching my breath and looking for the bodies. I'd lost them in the rain, but would a clear day betray their location? My teeth knocked together. My arms were tired. I went under one last time to confirm the job was done, pushing myself deeper until my feet finally stabbed into the silty lake bottom. Plants grabbed at me, but I batted them back. The water was deep, I had no doubts now. Given that, and the length of the rope, Ms. Klein and the boy were sure to be more than a few feet under. Deep enough for a canoe to pass over them, or even a swimmer.

Confident in my work, I kicked toward the surface until my head met something solid. It held me under the water like a palm as I pressed it with my hands, trying quickly to move it or to find an edge. I screamed whatever oxygen remained in my lungs and slammed my fists into the mass above me. A moment of clarity was delivered upon me as I struggled, and I realized that, were I to die here in this lake, joining the corpses of my teacher and the boy I did not know, the other boys at the facility would happily go on with their lives. There would be no search, as there hadn't been for Fry. The Headmaster might register my absence, but only as an inconvenience. He would frame the next new boy, or an old boy he'd grown tired of, and he would tell Hannan that he'd dealt with me in private.

I had no companions, no one to grieve for me. I had not had the impact I would have liked. I clawed at the oppressive shape and eventually found a seam. A long, narrow opening, which I realized was where the bodies met. The darkness at the edges of my vision grew, as I dug my fingers between the corpses, pulling at them and sliding my hand along each grisly feature, until I was suddenly, blissfully free.

THE GHOST

The garden hoe had been washed clean by the rain. I filled in the hole in the garden's plot, then gathered the other tools into the wheelbarrow, which was now bent slightly at the middle. Even so, getting everything back up the hill was comparatively light work.

The toolshed was sealed with a padlock upon my return. Clean and gleaming, spotted with rain. There'd been no padlock before. I'd heard nothing about a key. I had no doubt this was an obstacle intentionally set in my path by unknown schemers, pranksters, or the Headmaster.

I flipped the wheelbarrow so it wouldn't gather water. I set the tools under a jutting edge of the shed's roof. I glanced at the lake, which sat like a mirror on the horizon.

The other boys were in their rooms when I returned. I heard no tears through the doors, saw no fear at all on the faces of those whose doors had been left open. It would have been easy to assume these boys knew nothing of what had happened to the boy I'd been sent to the garden with, or to our teacher. But it was just as easy to suspect that some of them did know, that Hannan had in fact seen what I thought he might have seen, and that he'd told them by now, or at least some of them, in confidence or conspiracy. It was also possible he'd gone to the Headmaster in my absence. I was fine not knowing who my opponents were just yet, as I would find them all out eventually and deal with each, one by one. I was stronger than they might have imagined: Hannan, the Headmaster, or any other boys pitted against me. I had a young body, a keen mind, and an old soul. This would not go as easily as they hoped.

I walked the length of the hall, stopping just short of my room, where, through the opened door next to mine, I saw a familiar boy on his back in bed. I recognized him from the dishwashing line, as he was always on it. In fact, thinking of it, I realized I'd never seen him do any other work. I noticed now that he had a scar that ran across his chin, a thick line that marked the base of the jut. Though we shared a wall, though we slept only a short distance from each other every night, I couldn't remember us ever having actually spoken. I wasn't even sure if I knew his name. But because of his perennial place on the dishwashing line, I understood that the Headmaster didn't like him. For that reason, I felt close to this boy in that moment. I couldn't have guessed at what had gone on between the two of them, but whatever it was, I stood outside his door, reflecting briefly on the sadness of his existence. There had been a point in his life when people had looked at him and thought he might have done anything at all with himself. They would have seen nothing but potential in him, and it might have appeared to them, and maybe even to him, that anything and everything was within his reach. And now he worked the dishwashing line.

I took a breath. My mood was affecting my thinking. The truth was, I knew nothing of the boy's history, his family, the circumstances of his birth. He might have been born in a bucket, for all I knew, and dumped into the street from a third-story window. Maybe there'd never been any hope at all.

With that, my sadness evolved into actionable pity. *The poor boy*, I thought, *needs to be given a chance*. It's possible he's never had one. It's likely he is yearning for one, underneath his casual presentation. I couldn't imagine a better candidate for a comrade. Surely he wasn't satisfied with his lot in life, and a sense of belonging might in some small way renew his faith in himself, which had likely been scrubbed out after so many years on the dishwashing line.

I stepped into his room and shut the door behind me.

"Have you seen Hannan?" I said.

He didn't get up or look over. "I heard you drew naked pictures of Ms. Klein," he said.

"So you have seen Hannan," I said.

He blinked at the ceiling. "No," he said. "But he wasn't on the dishwashing line after lunch. I came straight here after. I've hardly seen anyone."

I shook my head. I grieved for this boy and felt strengthened in my resolve.

"I'd like to purchase one," he said.

"What would you like to purchase?" I said.

He sat up, checked the door to confirm it was shut. "One of your pictures," he said.

"I haven't drawn anything," I said. "And besides, the Headmaster has all the drawings in his possession, and I'm at the beginning of a punishment for their existence."

"I understand," he said. "I get it. But if you were to somehow find yourself in possession of one, a new one, say, I'd pay a decent price for it."

"You're a pervert," I realized.

"I'm Nick," he said. "I'm a young boy, and I'm lonely. And I am deeply in love with Ms. Klein. Are you so different?"

"Of the list," I said, "you and I share one attribute. But what would you consider a decent price?"

"I'd pay you two dollars for a quality drawing."

"Out of the question," I said, and I turned to leave.

"Five dollars," he said, "if I can see it first and determine the quality."

"You can see it for one moment," I said, "but you can't hold it or touch it."

"If you happen to come into possession of one, you mean," he said.

"Yes," I said, "if one finds its way to me."

I went to my room and drew a crude portrait of Ms. Klein, as I'd seen her. Only I straightened the fingers and imagined her hair flowing and full.

I brought the drawing to Nick only moments later. I shut the door again and held it up for him.

"It's terrible," he said.

"Now that we are in each other's confidences," I said, "I'd like to form an official alliance."

"But it isn't good," he said.

"People are dying," I said. "The bodies are stacking up. You haven't heard about it yet, I'm now sure, but you will soon enough. Everyone will. And when they do, people are going to start choosing sides. I'm ahead of the game. I have information no one else does. But I need someone on my side. I have a plan for how to get us all out of here safely and securely, while other people are going to pit us against one another in order to ensure their own survival. Those selfish brutes will be the people we are against in our alliance. It will be us versus them. We will be courageous and sympathetic, but strong and committed to our plan. What do you say?"

"Who is dead?" he said.

"There are two already," I said. "And I assure you the situation is likely to yield more by the end."

"How did they die?"

"They were murdered."

He went white.

"It's started," he said.

"Twice," I said.

"No," he said. "It's the ghost. There will be five."

"There's no such thing as the wandering dead," I said. "That's a contradiction. I need you to focus on what's happening, not what can be imagined."

He didn't respond. He was blank and pointed toward the heavens.

"Did you hear what I said?" I said.

"You have a plan to keep us safe?" he said without looking at me.

"I have the only plan that will work," I said.

"What's the plan, then?" he said.

"Buy the drawing to declare your loyalty," I said, "and we will put things into action immediately."

"But it doesn't look like anything," he said.

"It's a symbol," I said.

I did not have a plan, but I could now make room for one to develop. The others would surely come up with something fast, and the lot of us would divide according to our sense of who most promisingly assured survival. Prior loyalties could play some role in this division, but fear shatters loyalty, especially among young boys.

I paced the length of my small room, trying to understand what could be done. The rain had not let up. There was thunder and lightning now as well, but it could not reach me.

"Ha," I yelled at the ceiling, where the rain was being forced to stop.

The most urgent thing was to find Hannan. To find out what he knew. It was possible the Headmaster was hiding him somewhere. It was also possible the Headmaster had never sent him down to the garden at all. If the Headmaster was even madder than I'd originally imagined, if the teacher's murder hadn't in fact been the boiling over of a tumultuous and for-bidden affair but instead one episode in an ongoing nightmare perpetrated against the forgotten children abandoned to his care, it was likely he'd also done something to Hannan, adding that poor boy's disappearance to the suspicious circumstances he'd built up around me like a child playing with a beetle, setting down obstacles and forcing it to walk back and forth while slowly drawing those obstacles closer together until the beetle has nowhere left to crawl, has not even enough room to get its bloated body turned around to face the direction in which it had originally intended to go. Surely there was a way to keep the walls from closing in.

I had no sense of how long I'd been walking the lengths of my room, so I went to the window. The sky was dark and the building seemed to shake in the rain. I was outraged at being made to feel so helpless. I wasn't helpless at all. I wasn't a beetle. I wouldn't circle until it was too late and then expire. There were paths yet to imagine, and every plan houses infinite corruptions.

I sat at my desk and made several more pictures of Ms. Klein. I marched them to the Headmaster's office, where he was standing at the window, watching the storm. There was a low fire in the fireplace and I could hear the rain sizzling against the coals as it found its way down the chimney. A yellow foam pad wrapped in bungee cords sat by his desk next to several green military bags.

"There's lightning in the mountains," he said.

"These are the remaining drawings," I said, setting the fresh pages on his desk, where there was still a little pile of fully folded paper. "And my drawing materials," I said, handing over the pencils as well.

"Good," he said. He nodded at the window. "It presents a problem."

"That's all of them," I said. "There are no more. If any more turn up, they are not of my creation. You should know that

I've heard rumors of other boys taking up the same practice, though I've never seen it for myself. Do you believe me?"

He turned back to the desk, lifting the pages.

"You have a real talent," he said. "It's unfortunate this is the way you've chosen to express it. But I was a boy once. I understand the magnetic draw of nudity and violence. Though I'm putting a stop to it, that doesn't mean I can't see it as an understandable enough expression of the desires you might be feeling that you aren't sure what to do with. It's an important step you're taking toward mastering the strange forces of adolescence."

"Thank you," I said. I watched his scheming face.

"Can I trust you with an announcement?" he said.

"Of course," I said.

He lifted my pages from one side of the desk, walked around to the other, and opened a drawer from which he withdrew several more pages. He thumbed through them, an odd smile on his face. He lifted the other stack from the shelf behind his desk and flipped through it as well.

"Tell the other boys we are on lockdown for the foreseeable future," he said. "This weather system has made it over the mountains and settled into our small valley here. It's intensifying. It will get worse before it gets better. We had lightning accidents last year due to negligence on my part. I have accepted the blame and improved my strategy. They won't be happy to hear it. They're used to getting to play in the rain. They're used to taking the storms casually. But not this year. It's a lockdown, plain and simple, until further notice."

"What happens during a lockdown?" I said.

"I'll set up in my office," he said, kicking the foam pad.

"And no one is to leave the main building without my express permission. I've already dismissed Ms. Klein, and I will fill in for her for the time being. You'll all go to class and to the dining hall, where, until further notice, we'll eat what rations are stored in the kitchen. There will be no outside play and no visits to or from beyond the valley."

I did not flinch at the mention of Ms. Klein's dismissal. I stood my ground, swallowing stomach acid like saliva. If my eyes were watering, it was because of the smoke from the fire.

"When will it end?" I said.

He'd made his way over to the hearth, where he was crumpling the pages and tossing them casually into the flames. "When the weather changes," he said.

"How long will that take?" I said.

The fire snapped a coal onto the carpet.

"It was almost a month last time, but these storms do as they please. We just have to remain calm and be patient," he said, smothering the coal with the heel of his loafer.

He would fill in for Ms. Klein. It was brilliant. Despite the threat it posed to me, I had to admit the plan was a marvel to behold. He was a stunning opponent, the Headmaster, one perpetually a step ahead of me, operating just beyond the horizon of my thought. If I'd accepted responsibility for the drawings, thereby partially relieving the pressure he planned to suggest might have forced me to strike out against Ms. Klein, he would respond by tightening his grip (under the auspices of protecting us, no less), heightening the tensions inherent in the lots we'd been cast, the sorrowful day-to-day lives we each led in our prison of sorts, our desert island of castaway boys, so that it no longer mattered if he succeeded in framing me, as, at the end of all this, one of us, one of the boys in his charge, was sure to snap, or fold, or bend, or break, in a way that would benefit him and maybe help divert any suspicions cast his way. On top of that, if Hannan had in fact seen what happened in the garden, and if he had told the Headmaster about it, then I was not only a boy with evidence linking him to an obsessive relationship with the murdered Ms. Klein, but demonstrably a murderer of children. With me doubly damned, the Headmaster knew he could be calm and patient in his planning, and I would have to simply wait the matter out, responding to each new snap of the trap as it announced itself, as my guilt would make me fundamentally unreliable in the eyes of any potential investigators, not to mention in the eyes of my cohort.

While he could not have brought on the rains that evening, the Headmaster had certainly taken advantage of the opportunity they presented, as he seemed almost always to be able to do. I could see it in that moment with him by the fire. This, whatever *this* was, wasn't something that began with me, but something I had stepped into the middle of. My first day was in no way the first day qua first day, but some unremarkable middle day, hardly noticeable on the list of what had happened and what would happen, and the Headmaster had simply accommodated my presence in the way he accommodated all new additions, developments, or complications—that is, casually and effectively, because the Headmaster was either a mastermind of murderous behavior or, more likely, he'd been at it for so long that he was simply well-practiced in and comfortable with the complicated dynamics of executing the long-term, variable planning it required. I was sure that, prior to my first day, year after horrible year, he'd managed to come up with something to explain away whatever strange occurrences led to the disappearance of a boy, or a teacher, say, or anyone else upon whom he felt the axe must fall. How casually everyone had absorbed Fry's disappearance. And now, possibly, Hannan's too, as, if he hadn't in fact seen me in the garden and rushed directly to report it all to the Headmaster, thereby receiving sanctuary and being hidden for deployment at a later development in the plan, if he hadn't seen and done those things, then, it became suddenly clear to me, Hannan was simply missing. A cause for alarm. And regardless of what Hannan's true fate was, to the other boys, who it was possible had no idea of what had happened in the garden, to those boys, Hannan was simply gone. There was no sign of Hannan and no clear way for them to understand his disappearance. They didn't even have the comfort of a theory, which, I had to admit, I did, however menacing mine was. And yet there'd been nothing in the air of the dormitory to suggest that we'd lost yet another member of our cohort. Strange, indeed.

I went straight from the Headmaster's office to Nick's room, but the door was closed. I knocked, and when no one answered, I pounded. Still nothing. I crossed to the door opposite Nick's, which opened onto a room belonging to another young boy whose name I did not know, with a face I did not recognize. I entered without knocking and found him on his belly in bed. His head was where his feet should have been, and his top half was propped up, hovering over a book.

"Excuse me," I said. "I know we haven't been formally

introduced, but I need some information immediately and my preferred source won't open his door."

"We've met," said the boy.

"Be that as it may," I said.

"Anders," he said, shutting the book.

"Anders," I said. "Yes, of course. Anders. How could I forget Anders? The truth is that I didn't forget Anders, but was worried you might have forgotten who I was, and I didn't want to put any undue social pressure on you. It's not that you should remember me, after all. We've only met the one time."

"We've worked the dish line together," he said, "many times."

The dish line! I thought. The wretched dish line. When would we be done with it?

"I rarely work the dish line," I said. "You might be confusing me with another boy who's assigned to that station more often."

"I'm not confused," he said, reopening the book.

"Wait," I said, "we've gotten off on the wrong foot. I only need you to help me with one question and then I will leave, and if we are ever on the dish line together again, I promise to remember you."

"I don't care at all if you remember me," he said. "Rat."

"Rat!" I said. "On whom did I rat?"

"On whom?" he said. "On whom! Everything about you is false and misleading."

"I've only come to ask a question," I said.

"Well, you've done nearly everything but," he said.

It occurred to me that this boy was taking far too much pleasure in these distractions. Or, more than pleasure, he had the satisfied look of someone successfully executing an assigned task. It was as if the shape and purpose of our conversation had been predetermined, and he was merely cycling through the steps designed to keep me from ever asking my question outright, steps meant to hold me in the doorway churning through meaningless conversational loops that would keep me focused on him, moment to moment, and not on whatever else might be happening behind my back. And what might be happening behind my back? The only thing for certain was that there was no way of knowing while I was stuck in this room talking with this boy. It was a brilliant tactic, and I had to admire it.

"So, what's your question?" said the boy.

I slammed shut his door as I stepped into the hall and made quickly for my room. There was no one in it and nothing out of the ordinary. I searched the bed and found nothing planted. The drawers of the desk were empty, its surface bare. I checked the window and it was sealed; no one in the yard, no one on the walkways outside. I checked the dresser and found everything as it had always been.

I was calming down, beginning to realize that I might have overreacted. Everything in my room was safe and fine and exactly as it had been when I left it. And yet, for the sake of being thorough, I opened my narrow closet, which was roughly twice my height, and it was there that I discovered the corpse of Hannan.

THE GHOSTS

The corpse slid from the closet and I shoved it back in, slamming the door to pin it in place. While I did not recognize his face, it required little deductive work to determine who it was and what it was doing there. I'd been looking for Hannan. I'd made it known that I wanted to find him. It was possible to conclude that I wanted to find Hannan because he had seen what had happened in the garden. If I was the one who'd murdered Ms. Klein, and then the boy in the garden whose name I did not know, of course I would have no moral tremblings over tracking down and murdering the boy who would be able to testify to that effect. And that was Hannan, the boy who had clearly seen me punch the boy whose name I did not know in the garden, sending him down onto the garden hoe, which I'd washed in the rain and set by the toolshed. Incidentally, locking me out of the toolshed was yet another ingenious move on the Headmaster's part, as it guaranteed that particular garden hoe wouldn't be lost among the many other garden hoes. Perhaps due to the fact that gardening had once been included in the curriculum, the facility possessed an almost comical excess of garden hoes. Now the Headmaster, along with whichever boys he'd turned or forced into his confidences through either fear or some more complicated manipulation, had one of the three murder weapons set aside for them, still streaked with microscopic evidence, I had no doubt.

And now here was Hannan. Poor Hannan, who had only been trying to secure his own safety and comfort by affirming his allegiance to an unhinged Headmaster, coming to him with all he knew, all he'd seen in the garden. It was possible too that Hannan had not only seen me in the garden but had followed me over to the lake, where I'd disposed of the bodies. Reporting back to the Headmaster, he would have revealed that the bodies had been hidden, had been washed of evidence, and could not be brought out of the water without a great deal of effort and risk of exposure. These corpses were no longer corpses upon which anyone might stumble. More important, the extent of the physical labor required to hide them in this way was less suggestive of a young boy operating on his own than of a grown man, which would certainly be something the Headmaster would have difficulty explaining. It didn't make him guilty of the crime, necessarily, and it was true he could make the claim that Hannan had witnessed my part in it all and reported it back to him, but the nature of their disposal would certainly raise questions, making the whole thing far less clean than the original arrangement: one corpse unearthed in the garden. So Hannan had taken Ms. Klein's place as the corpse that could be and would be and had been stumbled upon, although perhaps not by the correct person. Either way, a boy who had possibly witnessed me taking the life of another boy and then disposing of two bodies was now dead. Poor Hannan, boxed in and bunched up against my closet door. It did not and would not look good.

There was a knock then, and the door began to open, so I dropped my trousers and took my penis in hand.

"A minute please," I said. "A minute."

The door shut quickly and I heard the sound of laughter, one boy's and then several.

"What do you need?" I yelled through the wood.

"We've brought you a gift," said a voice.

"Who is *we?*" I said.

"Radek, me, Klausen," it said.

"Who's me?" I said. I was trying to determine if I could fit Hannan's body through the window above my desk. It seemed possible, provided it wasn't too heavy. But I wouldn't be able to do it quickly. And once it was out there, then what? The corpse would sit in the rain, waiting to be discovered. The closet was a good hiding place for now, except for the fact that Anders and the Headmaster and God knows who else knew the body was there. It was even possible they were here now to collect, to push forward their terrible plan, and have the blame fall firmly, and once and for all, on me.

"Klot," said the voice.

"Klot?" I said. "Who is Klot?"

"Yes," he said. "Klot."

"Where are you from?" I said.

"Can we come in?" he said.

Even if Anders and the Headmaster were not among them, it was still possible these boys were part of the clever trap. I had to be cautious. I could assume nothing.

"I'll come out in a moment," I said.

"It's a sensitive matter," they said, speaking over one another in their rush to draw me out.

"Your gift?" I said.

I pulled up my trousers. I could hear them whispering but not what they were saying. I stepped toward the door, set my ear against the wood. They pounded, startling me back.

"We lied," said Klot.

I heard the laughter of several boys in a group. I've heard few things more chilling.

"Let's meet in your room, Klot," I said.

"I'm afraid we can't," he said, "because, you see, I've had to give up my room following the arrival of our thirty-first. We are low on beds, low on rooms. You couldn't lie on your back in the space I now occupy."

"What space do you occupy now?" I said.

I approached the door again and slid the lock into place as quietly as possible.

"I can hear you at the door," said Klot. "What do you think you're doing? Put yourself away and let us in."

"I'm afraid I can't do that, Klot."

"Because you're a helpless pervert?" said Klot.

"Because I'm ill," I said. "I'm physically ill."

I blew my nose, losing no phlegm.

"Let us in or we will let ourselves in," said Klot.

It was possible I could fit my own body out the window, but that would leave these boys alone in the room with Hannan, and if they didn't already know he was in there, I had no doubt they would find him if left to their own devices. And what then?

"What's this all about?" I said.

"A gift," said Klot.

"You said you were lying about that," I said.

He pounded against the door again. I could have sworn I heard its wood snap.

I unlocked the lock and opened the door just wide enough to fit my body through the crack, then slammed it shut behind me.

The hall was empty. There were no boys. There was no laughter.

"Klot," I yelled. "Klot! Everyone come into the hall. Klot has a gift for me."

Two boys came out of their rooms. One was the boy whose glasses would not stay on. He was having as much trouble with them now as he had been in the dining hall.

"What's all the noise?" said the other of the two.

"Where's Klot?" I said.

Both boys shrugged.

"Who?" said the boy whose glasses would not stay on.

"Never mind," I said. "I have an announcement."

"Calm down," said the same boy.

"It's urgent," I said. "Everyone! Out of the rooms."

Nick's door was still closed. My hope was that he was in there alone with the drawing and that nothing had come over him, nothing had happened to him, nothing had been done. The question of his safety made me wonder if I'd been foolish to trust him in the first place, to approach him at all, let alone with talk of some kind of plan. How brilliant would that have been, to plant an indifferent and calm-seeming boy on his back in bed so that I might approach him on my own? It wasn't beyond the Headmaster to dream up something like that. If I was right in all that he'd accomplished so far, it seemed only natural that he would install some kind of insurance, a side-net I might wander haplessly into without being guided. And how convenient that would be, not to have to guide me at all.

Anders stepped out of his room, the book tucked in his armpit.

"I have an announcement," I yelled again.

"Get on with it then," said Anders.

"It's for everyone," I said.

"Just say what it is," he said, "and it will make the rounds. If you even have something worthwhile to tell, that is."

Thunder clapped and the hall went black.

"Ha!" I shouted, at the ceiling, at the storm, at Anders and the other boys, who were, I was sure of it now, in cahoots.

I was wrapped in small hands then, confirming what I already knew to be the case. Anders, the boy struggling with his glasses, the boy I didn't know, Klot, Klausen, Radek: I could feel them all grabbing me at once, covering my mouth, holding my arms and legs still, lifting me and carrying me through the total darkness of the hall.

"Put me down!" I said.

70

And they eventually did, in a room the size of an upright coffin. I could feel the walls around me, holding me in place.

"It's yours now," said Klot, and I heard the door slam.

I felt the air in the room grow thick. I pounded my body against the concrete walls to the best of my ability in the cramped space. It made little to no sound. But the door was made of metal, and when I kicked it, it sang. I shouted and kicked and demanded release. Nothing changed and no one came. I pounded and pounded and pounded. I thought of Hannan. I thought of Ms. Klein. Both woundless. Both trapped. Was this how it had happened? Had the others just left them somewhere, walled up like the beetle? I was furious. I was disgusted. I was boiling over with rage.

"Please," I said. "Please."

Poor Hannan. Poor Ms. Klein. Poor, poor me. And then my heart went out to the boy I'd murdered. It just took off like a bird from a branch. The walls of my tomb seemed to fall away, and there was only darkness. I had ended his life. I had plucked it from his body with my own hands. With my angry fist. I could feel the weight of each death suddenly, as if I would drown in them. As if I was tied to a rock in a lake full of corpses. I gasped for air.

There was a thin chain above me, and it ticked against a lightbulb when I touched it. I pulled it and it clicked, but no light came. I pulled it again. I wiped my face. I pounded on the metal door until my hands felt bruised.

I was in the dark, collapsed against the rear wall of my prison, banging the back of my head there with a mournful rhythm, when the door clicked open. I braced myself to be wrapped in hands again, or to be struck.

"Are you coming or not?" whispered Nick through the darkness.

"Nick," I said. "You're out of your room. You're alive."

"Shh," he said. "Of course I'm alive."

"I haven't seen you," I said. "I haven't heard from you."

"I came by your room," he said.

"And you didn't hear me yelling?" I said.

"I heard you shouting in your room earlier, and I came then. When you were masturbating," he said.

"That wasn't you," I said. "That was Klot."

"I assure you," he said, "it was me."

"Either way, you've got it wrong," I said. "I wasn't masturbating. I was staging an intimate moment so whoever was walking in would be encouraged to leave immediately."

"But you told me to come by," he said.

"You should have announced yourself," I said.

"Who is Klot?" he said.

"That's why I like you, Nick. You are focused and you keep to yourself. Is that why you like me?" I said.

"You said you had a plan," he said.

"I do," I said. "A very good one. But new information has come to light and we need to go over it."

"Come to my room," he said. "Hurry."

He wasn't touching me yet, but I still felt somehow that I was being rushed.

"Where is everyone?" I said.

"They've left to get the candles," he said.

I can admit I was happy to see him, happy to have the door open and someone at my side, but it was clear something wasn't right.

"Nick," I said, "what took you so long to come and rescue me from the closet?"

"I came as quickly as I could," he said.

"Didn't you hear me crying out? Banging against the door?"

"I heard something," he said, "yes. But you can't always be sure you're hearing what you think you're hearing, and I've learned not to follow strange sounds into darkened corners."

"Wise enough," I said, "but then you came. What changed?"

"I thought we were allies," he said.

He was nothing but a voice in the darkness, but I was confident in my ability to imagine the tragic look on his scarred face in that moment.

"We are," I said, "to the bitter end."

"Then why does it sound like you don't trust me?"

"Nick," I said, "there is no one else I hold above you in terms of trust."

"Good," he said.

"And you trust me?" I said.

"You said you had a plan to get us out of here," he said.

"It's not safe to talk in these halls," I said. "We might trust each other, but that's as far as we should extend our trust for the time being."

"I understand," he said.

"Then let's head to the gazebo," I said. "We can talk in private."

"There's a storm," he said.

"We'll move quickly," I said. "It's darker in here than it is out there, and besides, the people who wish to do us harm have revealed themselves. They are among us. Take my hand, Nick. Help me out."

Nick took my hand and pulled me from my coffin. We traveled together through the dark hallway and to the exit. A dim light filled the entrance of our dormitory as the door opened, and rain found its way immediately to the floor. We dashed hand-in-hand through muddy grass and to the gazebo, which we could clearly see articulated against the blue backdrop of our stormy sky. Ripples of thunder were as constant as the ocean's waves, and lightning lit the scene like a wind-torn fire. It was elemental, like we were witnessing the Earth's creation. I felt a burst of energy, a charge that could be harnessed and used to bring down our enemies.

"Take it all in," I told Nick. "Soak it up."

He was catching his breath and watching the dormitory door to see if we'd been followed. It didn't move at first, but then it startled. I twitched at the sight, but nothing came. We'd left it open and the wind was getting around it.

Above us, the gazebo roof screamed with rain.

"Nick," I said. "Are you listening to me?"

"The door," he said.

"Forget it," I said. "From here, we can see everything coming. Nothing can surprise us. This is where we'll stay."

"For how long?" he said.

THE JOB OF THE WASP

Lightning throttled the darkness.

"Until we both understand what we have to do next," I said. "The important thing is to be calm and patient. We are not beetles."

"Okay," he said. "I know that."

THE GHOSTS AS THEY WERE
KNOWN TO NICK

Above us, the wasps weren't moving. I could see their frozen back ends jutting out of the nests along the corners of the gazebo's roof. Were wasps frightened of thunder? I wondered. How could they not be? What would thunder be like to something so sensitive and small? Then again, it was hard to imagine they were capable of feeling fear at all. They were wasps. I couldn't get my head around it in the moment. I wanted to understand them, but it was beyond me.

"Nick," I said, "do you believe it's possible for two living things to ever reach a place of mutual understanding?"

"You said you had a plan," said Nick.

"Of course I have a plan, Nick," I said. "I've gotten us this far, haven't I?"

"And where exactly are we?" said Nick.

"We're in a safe place," I said. "Alive and well."

"I was alive and well before our alliance," he said. "Everyone here is alive and well for now, and without even trying. Without getting themselves stuck out in a storm. The roads are covered in mud. The valley is filling with water. There's no way in and there's no way out. At least I had a bed before. So far, I've only lost comforts and gained nothing more by joining up with you."

It was time to put all my cards on the table, time to tell Nick everything I knew and to break the claw of ignorance that held him in its grasp.

"You mentioned a ghost before," I said.

Nick squinted.

"Tell me everything you know about it," I said.

"I only know what I was told," said Nick, "and what I suspect."

"Tell me what you were told," I said.

"Tell me your plan," he said.

"Why are you so hesitant to tell me what you know?" I said.

"Because I'm getting nervous," he said. "I'm cold and I'm frightened."

"You should be nervous," I said. "You should be frightened. But you have to trust me, Nick, or this alliance is going to fall apart."

I could see in his face that he knew it was true. There was a sadness there, which I recognized as the deep existential turmoil of a child who has realized how little control he has over his own life, and that the mature thing to do is not to face every challenge alone but to put his trust in another. It was understandable for a boy whose early development had been frustrated by years spent almost exclusively on the dishwashing line, that he would want to finally take charge in this moment of chaos and freefall, but our survival depended on him curbing his impulse to lead and accepting his lesser, though no less honorable, fate as my partner.

"My parents died in a fire," he said.

"How sad," I said, glancing at the frozen back ends of the wasps. It was possible, I realized, that they were all dead. The temperature had dropped considerably when the storm settled on us, and it was reasonable to assume the sudden drop would shock their little systems. Maybe they'd seen it coming. Maybe they'd all gathered in their nests together for those final moments. I'd always imagined wasps were the evilest insects in the insect world. They were manipulators, liars, imposters. They had narrow little stinging faces. But imagining them all gathered together in the wind of the oncoming storm, their bodies swelling the edges of the sockets of their shared home, I felt a sudden respect for them. I felt immensely sad for what had become of them, and moved by their solidarity, their unity in the most difficult of times, at least for a wasp. The boys in the facility would likely never have this level of devotion to one another. We had been at each other's throats from the day of my arrival. If I'd had a plan, as I was sure I soon would, they wouldn't follow my lead. Even for Nick, who may very well have had the best intentions, it was a struggle. And all were doomed because of it.

The dormitory door slammed against its frame but did not shut.

"After that," he said, "I was an orphan, charged to the state. They kept me in a large facility filled with other orphaned boys."

"Like this place," I said, watching the door and then the wasps.

"No," he said. "This place is heaven compared. The other facility was much taller, but it had no outside areas in which we could play. There were hundreds of boys housed there, and nearly all of them were sick. Coughing up their sleeves, vomiting into buckets. It was horrid. I came down with what they kept calling a 'terminal case.' At first I was coughing black bile into the buckets, then it was blood. Two men brought me into a room and discussed my condition. They decided that if it was indeed terminal, they would get rid of me before I passed on. They wouldn't be stuck with the bill for funeral arrangements or transporting the body. They wouldn't be stuck with the paperwork and the stigma of having lost yet another boy. I would need to be transported, they agreed, to another facility. A smaller facility that could provide the kind of attention I would surely need as my condition worsened. Somewhere outside of town, where I could see the hills and the sunsets and the lakes and maybe live out my few final months in peace. They were not talking to me. They were making a plan for me. I was loaded into a cart and brought here."

"You don't seem sick," I said.

"That's the thing," said Nick. "I got better."

Thunder struck.

"I can't explain it. I was here for several weeks, feeling miserable and vomiting blood, as I had always been. And then one morning, I woke up with a clear head. My lungs were sore, but I wasn't forced over to the bucket. Not even once. I attended class. I even began to play with the other boys. My life felt entirely different. I haven't had so much as a cold since."

"What is the point of all this?" I said.

"When my parents died," he said, "my outlook on the world changed."

"You began to see it all as a maelstrom of life and death, a vast chaotic harmony in which the turning of a leaf carries no more significance than that of a human life," I said.

"No," said Nick. "I decided to believe in ghosts."

"You decided?"

"There is no knowing either way, correct?"

"Unless you've seen a ghost," I agreed.

"Okay," he said. "So, I began waiting to see a ghost. I started *expecting* to see ghosts. It became clear to me that there are only two ways of living: assuming there is no such thing as ghosts, or anticipating the possibility of seeing a ghost—that is, including the possibility of seeing ghosts in the way you think about the future. With two parents in the ground, I decided the latter was preferable. Why pretend to know what I was sure I didn't? Why assume anything? So I waited for them. I opened myself up to the possibility of ghosts. And as soon as I'd done that, things changed in very unexpected ways."

I examined the floor of the gazebo for a small rock or a bit of wood.

"I began to see things," he said. "Hear things."

"Such as?" I said.

"Voices," he said. "Shapes and figures."

"Here at the facility?" I said.

"Everywhere," he said. He narrowed his eyelids. "They're everywhere."

"But what of the ghost here at this facility?" I said. I was growing impatient with Nick and increasingly curious about the wasps, which were still not moving. I wanted to determine, once and for all, if they were as achingly beautiful as they seemed, and the only way of doing that was to disrupt their corpses, to knock them down with something and see what became of them. Would they empty hollowly from their sockets, or would they swarm?

"What is known," said Nick, "is that the facility is haunted. Every year, I've been told, the ghost sends five of us to Hell in its place, so that it can remain among the living. I have never seen the ghost, but I have felt its presence. Other boys claim to have seen the ghost, but it's been difficult to verify those claims. Last year, most believed we'd dealt with it. But I've still felt its presence. Perhaps you have too."

"What makes the claims difficult to verify?" I said.

"They don't line up," he said. "Each describes the ghost differently. Sometimes the ghost is young, a boy like any of us. Other times the ghost is an old man or an old woman in a green shawl. It depends on who's saying what on which day, or how the mystery manifests itself. It's very hard to come to an understanding of the dead based on details gathered exclusively by the living." He looked to the ground. He seemed to hold his breath for a moment. "The accusations do get out of hand," he said, "and it is frightening when it happens."

"Perhaps there are multiple ghosts," I said.

"It's possible," said Nick. "I won't argue with it."

"You know very little, Nick," I said.

"There is very little of which I can be confidently certain," he said.

"Nick," I said, "empty your pockets."

"What for?" he said.

"For the plan," I said.

He turned his pockets inside out, emptying thread and an eraser onto the floor of the gazebo.

I lifted the eraser.

"How will it help?" said Nick.

I weighed it in my hand.

"You don't have anything else?" I said.

He shook his head.

"Is that all there is to know about the ghost?" I said. "You're sure?"

"Not exactly," he said.

"What else is there?"

"There is our theory."

"Which is?" I was now furious with Nick for the way he was measuring out our time. "Just tell me all the information, Nick."

"It's not information, exactly," he said. "Only thoughts."

"I'm not going to ask again," I said.

"Some of us believe that the other boys are lying about having seen the ghost," he said. "While others think they are simply confused, or have been provoked to reckless speculation by the unverified accounts. We are even more skeptical of one another than usual because each maintains his own experience to be closest to the truth, drawing discrepancies into a harsh light. We've all witnessed something out of the ordinary at one point or another, but it is difficult to distinguish between the elements that truly comprise our shared experience here and the extra-real moments we experience only as individuals. Where is the line between the world we share and the worlds that exist exclusively for each of us? It's difficult to believe anything anyone says. Add to that the fact that every strange detail can ultimately be explained away by someone else, often in more ways than one, and the truth behind each account feels so far out of reach that we are perpetually in a situation where everything known has been described and yet nothing has been resolved."

I thought of the laughter outside my window then, and the absence of any determinable source. I thought of Klot, Radek, and Klausen, and how quickly they had vanished. Then the hands on my face, the hands I'd felt wrapped around me. It was true that if I presented my story as I'd experienced it, it would be a hard sell. But I was different from the other boys as Nick described them. I could admit I was without some critical information, and that my experience only accounted for a portion of the truth. Though my experiences might resonate with those who believed they were being haunted, I would never contend, based on what I'd been through, that I was being haunted. And though my story might have seemed unbelievable at times, I knew I wasn't making things up. I was not prone to flights of fancy. There were explanations available, if we were willing to pursue them. Gaps or no, I could see most of the world for what it was. I could see other people as they were, and I knew what they were capable of.

"When you say other boys were dragged back to Hell," I said, "what do you mean exactly?"

"I mean they disappear," he said.

"Sent away," I said. "Graduated. Buried." I could fill a book with more reasonable explanations than his.

"Maybe," said Nick. "We've never heard for certain either way."

"It's a long leap from there to ghosts," I said.

"For some," said Nick.

I felt relieved by the weakness of Nick's suspicions and resolve. It was almost funny to me, how easily he'd lost sight of the world to the visions in his head. Nick had a long, sad life ahead of him. He would live forever in his small room, haunted by the ghosts in his mind. Awaiting the arrival of transparent parents, perhaps still ghastly from their accident. No, it wasn't funny. It was tragic.

"Some boys go missing," he said, "and other days we simply can't keep the head count straight. We all seem to be there, but the numbers we remember don't add up."

"Thirty-one," I said. "Unless Fry has been sent home. Then we are thirty."

"There it is," said Nick. "If you'd asked me, I would have said we were twenty-eight."

"Well, you would have been wrong, Nick. That's the long and short of it. I was told the number by the Headmaster himself."

"Thomas and I did a count the day before you arrived," he said, "and we both counted twenty-eight."

"Who is Thomas?" I said.

"You know Thomas," he said. "He was on garden duty with you just this afternoon."

Had he winked just then? It was impossible to say. Had he grinned? If he had, it had been quick. Just a flash and then nothing. He was a master of deception or a dull boy lost to the past.

"I never learned his name," I said. "I am still getting settled here."

"After all this time?" said Nick. "Don't you find that strange?"

"New faces and new places," I said.

He nodded. "We all have trouble keeping track sometimes."

"Where is Thomas now?" I said. "Could we get him on our side before things start to go south?" I watched his face for anything out of the ordinary. I saw nothing definitive, but the restraint he exhibited in such a confrontational moment might alone have been evidence to his deceptive nature. Still, it wasn't enough to confirm it.

"I haven't seen him since he left with you for the garden," said Nick. He had turned his body to face me head-on. He had his hands out of his pockets, his arms bowed slightly at his side.

"Well, I saw him for some time after that," I said. "And I saw him return to the dormitory."

"What a few of us have come to believe," said Nick, "what we can agree on, based on all the contradictory accounts and missing details, is that the ghost walks among us."

"Oh?" I said.

"What makes the most sense," he said, "based on all that we know, is that one of the boys in our cohort is not a boy at all but a spirit haunting these halls."

"An interesting thought, there's no doubt," I said. "But if you could pick a place to haunt for eternity, would you choose this place?"

"Maybe you can't pick," he said.

"Maybe not," I said.

"Can I tell you a secret?" he said.

I nodded, curling my hand around the eraser to make a fist.

"For the longest time," he said, "I thought it was me."

"You seem very much alive," I said.

"But you didn't know me before," he said. "You've only met me this way. I was a mess before. And then suddenly so much better? It was like I'd passed through some screen and into an entirely different life altogether. Death, maybe. Or so went the story I proposed to myself every night before bed."

"But not anymore," I said. "Now you have a new theory."

We were circling one another. The lightning would flash every so often, revealing how pale he'd become. How sick he was with fear.

"You know," I said, "I'm not yet convinced you're entirely well."

"Maybe not," he said. "But I believe in the importance of staying open to possibilities that exist outside the realm of reason, though it more often than not results in our believing exclusively in what we hope for ourselves. For that reason, I also believe in the need to thoroughly and honestly examine one's beliefs and the true nature of oneself."

Our eyes locked.

"As a result," he said, "I can confidently declare that I am not our facility's ghost. I have checked my veins for blood, and I've found it."

He held up his wrists, which were plaid with scars.

"Bully for you," I said.

We no longer circled. We watched one another, frozen in our positions.

"Do you know whose veins I haven't checked?" he said.

I hurled the eraser at a wasps' nest then, beneath which our circling had positioned my new adversary. Either by luck or my natural athleticism, the nest received the full blow from the eraser, snapping its fragile stem and sending it down from its protected corner to the wooden floor of the gazebo, where it split.

Nick grinned when nothing happened. Then the wasps came twitching out and swirling up around him like a dust storm. Darting into the rain, I heard him howl as they began to sting.

I ran for the ivied trellis on the far side of the yard. I could hear the wasps buzzing every step of the way, and Nick's howling from underneath their defenses. If I'd been impressed with the wasps in what I'd imagined were their final moments, I was surprised to feel only a faint echo of that after seeing them swarm together and attack. There was something compelling about it, but it was far from beautiful. A coordinated attack, I realized, is less poetic than a mutually accepted defeat.

It had been clear all along that Nick wasn't a good ally. Too suspicious from the beginning. Too mad, too desperate, too singled-minded. But as Nick was chained to the fantasies that got him through the day, so I had been, holding out hope for Nick.

Who was left? A bunch of boys I didn't know and at least a

few enemies. A few enemies, I suddenly realized, I'd left alone in the dorms, with access to my room and to Hannan.

That was the end of it. My last bit of hope gone. The final wall was in place, and the boy now caught. There was nothing left to discover, no paths yet explored, and I ran, recklessly, hopelessly, through the rain until, in a proper end to a desperate night, I lost my footing and slid in the mud just shy of the ivied trellis, tearing a thigh-length split in the baggy left leg of my trousers.

PREPARING FOR PRISON

Under the trellis, the ivy dripped rain from its tendrils. I could no longer hear Nick's howls. Only the storm against the faulty roof over my head. I thought of what Nick had said, of how foolish he'd sounded in his resolve. He hadn't been a part of any grand plan. He wouldn't have been brought over to anyone's side, into anyone's confidences, as he was unpredictable, having abandoned his reason in favor of imagination and hope. He had been broken by his suffering, and in my desperation I might have related to him if his all-too-visible flaws had not served as guideposts in that moment, helping me steer myself back toward a more careful consideration of the facts.

What did I actually know, I wondered, and what was I just telling myself? There was Ms. Klein in the garden, who had started it all. Or, more accurately, there was Ms. Klein murdered in the garden, and her murderer who had started it all. Then there was Thomas, whose death had been an accident, but for which I was nonetheless to blame. Then there was Hannan, bunched up in my closet. Or, it was more than likely at this point, splayed out on the floor of my room, either

by design or as the unexpected result of a search by some un-
knowing party.

As ill-intentioned as they might have been toward me, I
had to admit it was more than likely that at least a few boys
were not working with the Headmaster. He couldn't have gotten to them all, and it wouldn't have made sense for him to try.
There had to be boys who were still after nothing more than
a little food and a roof over their heads, who had no idea how
bad things had become or how much worse they were about to
get. Those boys, it was clear to me, were in danger, and without
the opportunity to prepare themselves. If no one else would
help them, I understood the responsibility fell squarely on me,
which was maybe, I felt, a lot to ask of a child. After all, it
wasn't so long ago that I'd been like them, before our troubles
had revealed themselves with ghastly immediacy. While it
would be hard to call me innocent at this point, it seemed only
a moment ago when I'd been just that: innocent. I didn't want
to be responsible for protecting them; I wanted to be them. I
grieved for a time when I wasn't embroiled in a deadly conspiracy. When my hands weren't yet bloodied. When my story
was without dishonesty or suspicion, and when my primary
concern had been for the fit of my trousers.

My spirits had split with my pant leg. The energy provided
by my victory over Nick had carried me here, but I now sat on
the bricks of the walkway under the trellis, somehow feeling
defeated. I turned to face the lake, and when the lightning finally came, I could see the water in the distance like a fat black
pit. Was this what life was like for everyone else in the world,
or only what had been prepared for me? I knew the other boys,
however innocent, would be caught up in all this soon enough,

and I saw in that plain fact how little control I had over the way things went. Most things, at least. The important things. In that moment, the events of my life seemed nothing more than a series of random occurrences, the majority of which were in opposition to my desires, hopes, and plans. I broke a bit of ivy from its support and threw it toward the rain. The wind picked it up and hurled it back at me, which only confirmed my theory.

My theory. I laughed. I couldn't stop myself from laughing. One slip, one tear in my trousers, and I was overwhelmed. How typical of me to simply give up and call life impossible, rather than actually fight for what I knew was right. How easy I was making it on myself, I thought, peeling the wet ivy from my trouser leg so I could stuff its shredded ends into my sock. No. Life wasn't random and impossible. I smoothed the ivy in my palm and examined its veins. Whoever was behind this unraveling scheme had made a plan and put it into action. Things might have come up that they hadn't anticipated, but they had adjusted to meet the new challenges. They had adapted. Life was worse than random: It was something I wasn't good at.

I had tried to take control of the situation and I had failed. Or I had taken some control but not enough. Nick had been about to strike, and I'd dealt with it. That was true. But now he was out there, confirmed in his suspicions of me. I had only made things worse for myself in the long run. Ghost or no, I wasn't his ally. I never had been.

Poor Nick. We might have been stronger together. If he'd fallen in line, Nick and I could possibly have been a force to reckon with. But I now had to add Nick to that ever-expanding list of people who would like to see something terrible happen to me. The boys I was now responsible for were still boys who wanted to hurt me, either for what they believed had happened to Fry (it occurred to me then that Fry was likely dead too, hidden somewhere and waiting to be discovered by me in a vulnerable or hopeful moment) or for no reason at all other than that they were malicious boys or non-malicious boys with nothing better to do. Add to that the fact that I had no means of differentiating those boys from the boys under the Headmaster's influence. How many times had my generosity of spirit allowed craftier beings to gain the advantage?

The Headmaster himself had once acted supportive and firm, like a potential friend, someone who believed in me. As a result, I'd been open with him. I'd gone and done what he asked. I'd wanted him to like me, I admitted to myself, and not without shame. But in truth he had only ever seen me as an overweight patsy, someone on whom he could pin his crimes so that he might go on living as he had been, overseeing a facility populated with barbaric and perverted young boys, one of whom or many of whom, according to Nick, might be stuck in some purgatory of adolescence.

I watched the yard filling with muddy water. The unrelenting storm. How recently we had all been gathered there together, in the middle of a prank's unfolding, like any normal gathering of boys. We weren't piled in closets then, or tied to rocks in lakes. I could never have anticipated the horrors that had since occurred, or the horrors I'd since committed, and would now forever, I realized, have committed. How could I live with what I knew and what I'd done? Was there any potential use to the suffering I'd endured, or was there nothing left for me to do but reluctantly live out the final stages of a nefarious plot crafted by a homicidal despot who'd outsmarted me?

I reviewed what I understood of the Headmaster's plan. He had murdered Ms. Klein. He had selected the new boy to frame for the murder. Using the drawings, he would establish the new boy's obsession with his teacher. A disturbing obsession that had grown dangerous when it became clear it would never be a reality.

"I found the boy's drawings and I confronted him," the Headmaster might say, "and the following morning Ms. Klein didn't show up in the teachers' lounge. I searched the premises and discovered a young boy, Hannan, whom I had sent down to fetch the new boy from the garden, murdered and folded up in that same boy's closet. I instituted a facility-wide lockdown and searched the rest of the premises. I can't begin to describe the horror and shock I felt when we dragged the lake, only to discover Ms. Klein and young Thomas just beneath the surface, so coldly and deliberately dispatched."

They would find the garden hoe leaned against the toolshed, confirming the murder of Thomas during afternoon chores. By a boy of calculated genius and remarkable strength, they might say. A terrifying force. They might marvel at my ability to perform all those acts on my own, but it wouldn't necessarily shake their by now firmly evidenced belief that I was responsible. As Nick and I had only just proven, once an idea has taken root, however ill-founded, it is nearly impossible to weed.

Remarkably, going back over the details was already beginning to affect my mood. If a plan, however malevolent, could be so cleanly and assuredly executed, after all, there was hope to be found in that. On the other hand, if life was indeed random, or at least beyond my control, I needn't rely on hope to believe that things could suddenly change, or even possibly work out in my favor.

Thunder worked its way over the mountains, and a new strategy presented itself.

I'd only been feeling sorry for myself there under the trellis, detailing my own failures and fluctuating between self-hatred and despair. As the brilliant strategist behind my complicated but relentlessly effective framing had demonstrated, when things don't go according to plan, the plan can change. There is no right way to do a thing; there is only doing it and not. That I could even carry this thought revealed to me that I had not yet given myself up in full to nihilism, to the apparently unrestrained chaos of the world. Living was not impossible, no; it was difficult. I knew this. I had thought it before, but every thought requires repetition, as it takes time for the grooves of our fundamental beliefs to fully form.

I lifted myself up from the stone walkway. If I was being framed, let them frame me. How different could a prison for young boys be from this place? At the very least, I would have the opportunity to try again. To pay a little more attention and get a few boys onto my side early on. I could stand up for myself a little more the next time around. I could be better. I'd hardly been a presence at this facility, and it had chewed me up and spit me out. The world of young boys as I'd observed it favored action, and I'd hardly acted. I'd been acted upon, time and time again, and I decided then and there that it was time to stop playing defense. There were no ghosts here. Only a group of careless boys, brimming with unbridled power and perversion, and a man who had taken it upon himself to use them as he pleased. This was not the final chapter in my life but a turning point near the middle. One of what I was now sure would be many.

The difference between a boy and a man, I thought, was in whether or not he is able to find a way of taking control of his destiny. Or, at the very least, the difference lay in whether or not he was capable of living as if he might be able to take control of his destiny. Taking responsibility for himself while letting things come as they may. As Nick had chosen to live the rest of his life believing that ghosts were real, I would live the rest of my life knowing that there would be moments of control and there would be moments when control was wrenched from me. Regarding the latter, I had to be like the thunder rolling over the mountains. I had to match whatever force was acting against me and adapt accordingly.

It was a straight line from the trellised walkway to the corridor running between the dining hall and the dishwashing area, on to the Headmaster's office. When I opened the great wooden doors that connected the walkway to that hall, I heard a sound like the squeaking of a hinge or the laughter of a young boy. It hardly mattered, I decided, at that point, what it was. I would not be distracted by guesswork any longer. My torn and baggy pants were bloated with rain, and I left puddles wherever I stepped on my way toward accepting things as they were. The light was on in the Headmaster's office. I could see it in the crack under the door. The knob, however, would not turn, so

I knocked and waited. Seconds passed. I tried the knob again and was still unable to get it to turn. I knocked and waited a little longer.

"Sir," I said. "Sir, I've come to confess to more wrongdoing."

I was met with silence. Or, more accurately, I was met with the sound of thunder and the howling of the wind. Rain stabbed at the windows behind me. I placed my cheek against the door.

"Sir," I said. "I murdered Thomas. I didn't mean to, but nonetheless. I found Ms. Klein in the garden too. And poor Hannan in my narrow closet. Also, I set the wasps on Nick in the gazebo. If he's allergic to stings, it has just occurred to me, it's possible I've murdered him as well."

Thunder struck.

"Sir," I said. I knocked again. I slammed my body against the door.

It made a cracking sound but it did not budge.

"Sir, I've come to confess."

There was a bench opposite the Headmaster's office, where we would wait for our appointments. It was heavy, but I managed the task by lifting from my legs. I hurled the bench at the door, but it did not give way. I hadn't been able to get much force behind the bench, it's true. Though I could lift it, hurling it was a different story altogether. I moved the bench aside and tried with my body a few more times.

"Sir," I said.

It was possible he'd gone home for the night. Maybe the storm was clearing up and he'd received a report that it was okay to leave us on our own. Maybe help was on the way. If I was going to turn myself in, it seemed I would have to march my way down past the garden and the lake to the Headmaster's home on the edge of the property. I recalled the description he'd offered on the night of the prank. A fireplace, his wife with a cup of something warm. Maybe a fat black dog at the hearth. It was unsettling to imagine all that comfort provided him. One can't paint a picture of where a murderer will come from, I realized, only where murderers have come from in the past.

"Sir," I said. "Sir, I'd like to cooperate."

"What's all the noise then?"

I recognized Anders and the boy who was having trouble with his glasses, but not the two other boys with them. They were at the end of the hall in their pajamas, approaching me at a rapid pace.

"I can't get into the Headmaster's office," I said.

"Why do you need to get in there?" said Anders.

"I need to speak with him," I said.

"It can wait," said Anders. "You've got a lot of speaking to do before the night's through, and you can settle up with us first."

Nick turned the corner of the hall next, approaching from the door that led to the dorms. The same wounds that decorated his face were on his hands and feet.

"You've got to answer for what you did to Nick," said one of the boys I didn't know.

"He was about to attack me," I said. "I did what I needed to do to secure my safety."

"You haven't exactly done that," said the other boy.

"You left him out there," said the first, "to suffer on his own."

I realized then that, though they had different haircuts and one's pajamas were more faded than the other's, they had the same little face. They were twins, and I was curiously happy for them. Allies were hard to come by in our facility. They at least had each other, when so few of us had anyone.

"If I can talk with the Headmaster," I said, "all of this will be settled. I'll be sent away."

"We wouldn't want that to happen just yet," said Nick.

When they weren't speaking, I thought I could hear fluttering, like the wings of a bird trapped beneath an awning.

"Okay," I said.

"Okay what?" said the boy whose glasses were still sliding down his face.

"What's your name?" I said.

"Mine?" he said.

"Yes," I said.

"Why does it matter?" he said.

"I suppose it doesn't," I said. "But I wish you would share it."

They set upon me. Anders was the first to reach me, and I landed a punch to his gut, doubling him over. I then squared off with the first twin but foolishly turned to match the other twin as he made his way around me. I knew it was wrong, but only a moment after doing so, when the first twin had grabbed me from behind, followed soon by the boy who would not tell me his name, and then Nick. The twin I'd turned to match landed a few punches to my neck and the side of my head. They brought me down to the floor, and someone I could not see produced a rope. They bound my hands together, then bound that bundle to my ankles, so I was tied up like an archer's bow. They weren't hitting me any longer, so I stopped struggling.

"Sir," I yelled to the Headmaster's door.

"It's late," said Anders. "He's gone home. This stays between us for now."

They carried me down the hall like a roast.

"Nick, you have to tell them the truth," I said.

"You lied to me," said Nick.

"I never did," I said.

"You locked yourself in the closet and told me someone had done it to you," he said. "You told me we were in trouble."

"We are in trouble," I said.

"No," he said, "you are."

"That's enough," said Anders. "What would you like to do with him, Nick?"

We were at the door leading back out to the trellised walkway.

"Me?" said Nick. "I don't know."

"We're doing this for you," said Anders, "so you'd better come up with something."

"We could throw him into the lake," said one of the twins.

"Please," I said. "Please do not do that."

"We're not trying to kill him," said Anders. "You two are so twisted."

The other twin was smiling, I just knew it, but I could only see the floor above which I was suspended. No one had been sweeping. Or not well. There was dust and hair there, the husks of beetles and crumpled flies. Our building was a mausoleum.

"Let's take him to the gazebo," said the boy who would not tell me his name. "There are more nests there, right? We could knock a few down and leave him. Tit for tat. What do you say, Nick?"

"What if they don't sting him?" said Nick.

"They'll sting him."

"But how do you know?"

"They stung you, didn't they?"

Nick said nothing. I imagine he touched his face.

"All right," said Anders. "I think it's a fine plan. He'll get the message and wear the scars as reminders, won't he? It seems even."

"I already understand," I said to the floor, "and I will remember."

"You see?" said Nick. "It hardly matters to him."

"He deserves to suffer," said one of the twins.

"That's the point of punishment," said the other.

"You misunderstand me," I said. "I'm sure it will hurt a great deal. I'm sure I will suffer, and it will matter to me. I'm not without fear. I have simply accepted my fate. This is a turning of the tides. You will leave me in the gazebo and I will be stung and it will hurt. I'll be decorated with bloody wounds, just like poor Nick. The punishment is poetic in its echo of the crime. It won't matter to you to know that I didn't intend to hurt Nick at the beginning. That I never misrepresented myself to him, except in saying that I had a good plan for our escape. It's true that I didn't have a good plan; I only knew that we needed to escape. I have discovered a number of corpses around the property. We are each of us in mortal danger, I assure you. But I have had a change of heart in my approach. I am accepting things as they are, embracing my fate and whatever turns may come. Take me to the gazebo. Leave me if you like. I will rise again and go on with my plan. It doesn't matter what you do to me now, unless you throw me in the lake and leave me to die. But I can tell from the way we've just been talking that you aren't murderers. At least not the majority of you. You don't want me dead. You want me to pay for what I've done, and I accept that. I understand that you want to avenge your friend, to ease his mental anguish at having been bested in battle. I can't talk you out of it. I won't ask for mercy. Your plan will go exactly as you planned it. I will not interfere. And then the next thing will happen."

"Is that a threat?" said Anders.

"Not at all," I said. "I only mean to say that I am leaving this place. It might take longer than I'd like, but unless I'm in the ground before I do so, I am leaving. We aren't safe here, as I've said. We won't be until the larger matter is put to bed, and the only way I see that happening is to leave, so I accept whatever terms are necessary for that to happen. This isn't ultimately about Nick's wasp stings but the corpses gathering upon the grounds of our facility. I can only imagine what is behind the Headmaster's locked door, waiting to be discovered. Did you hear that fluttering? Did you hear that muffled and ungodly sound coming from the office? Why was the door locked? Why is no one coming to answer it? Something has to be done. All of this must come to an end."

They carried me through the rain to the gazebo, where they set me on the floorboards and knocked each of the wasps' nests down with a long branch. Anders was stung on the cheek, and the boy whose glasses were giving him trouble was stung on the leg during the process. They left me there, the wasps swarming above me, and headed back into the dormitories. It was a tragically innocent act. They were young boys doing all that was in their power to take control of their lives. The wasps hovered above me loudly and angrily. I could see the bright angles of their eyes, the curves of their pointed ends. They flew almost drunkenly, zigging and zagging, dipping down to my tied-up body. They crawled the lengths of my legs and arms, explored the caverns of my nostrils. The beaches of my ear. I could hear them clicking, as if they were talking to one another in some alien language. I watched the nests on the ground as more and more wasps poured out, rising up to the eaves in search of another place to rest.

I felt pity for them. There was no home left for them to reach. No place to which they could return. They would have to start fresh or die trying. But at least they had that option. It was my understanding that they built their nests from spit, though it's possible I was wrong. Either way, they'd done it once and they would do it again. Their homes were objects built, not things inherited. We orphans weren't so lucky. If our nest was knocked down by a murderous Headmaster, where was there left for us to go? Who would care for us? Who would take us in? I imagined that the wasps walking the edges of my body were simply looking for food or warmth. They weren't there to sting me. They weren't even angry any longer, it seemed to me. The other boys had left me, and though some wasps returned to the busy work of piecing together what was left of their lives right away, others abandoned hope momentarily to this warm lump on the gazebo floor, as a boy might collapse on a hillside under the baking sun or bang his head against a concrete wall.

I listened to the rain, which was beautiful in its unceasing assault.

"Thank you," I said, lifting myself from the gazebo floor.

The ropes fell away as the wasps on my body lifted. It broke my heart, how tragically fragile were the knots of my cohort. If they'd been there to hear me sigh, they might have known some part of my true feelings for them. I watched the wasps as they left me. Some brave souls rose to meet their brothers in the hunt for a new home, while others dropped to the floor, where they continued their pathetic crawl. Others yet landed in the curls of my hair. I brushed them out with my palm and sent them on their way. Somehow, incredibly, the wasps and I had reached an understanding. I meant them no harm, that first nest aside, and they knew it. They weren't interested in me other than as a surface. Something along which to move in their pursuit of safety for themselves and the rest of the hive. They were finding their way back to the life they knew and understood. I realized then that, though the other boys were predisposed to dislike me, and some of them were under the thumb of our murderous Headmaster, what they had been trying to do all along was this very job, the job of the wasps. I had disturbed the equilibrium of the facility, and they had been trying to set things right, just as Anders and his cronies had done by leaving me here to get stung. They were after their home again.

I left the gazebo and traveled through the rain back to the dormitories, where the power was still off. Candles had been lit, casting pools of golden light onto several low tables and desks that had been dragged into the hall. Several of the boys were sitting together in the dim light, talking or playing cards on the floor. They seemed almost peaceful, though they still startled when the thunder struck, and when the door slammed shut behind me.

REVOLT

"Boys," I said. "Brothers. Please listen to me."
A few of them turned away from their games. I realized I didn't know a single face of those in the hall. I made a vow to myself to be more attentive. To ask more questions. To try to listen. To write down names if I had to. *Imagine the kind of man you could be,* I thought. *Imagine all you could accomplish.*

"I have a confession to make," I said.

"You finished off the butter?" said one of the two boys playing cards.

I shook my head.

"You can't stop masturbating?" said the other.

Anders stepped out of my room then, and into the hallway. His face was pale. His lips were moving.

"I haven't allowed myself to become one of you," I said. "I haven't opened myself up to the use in our numbers, to the sheer force of a group of determined individuals, regardless of their names or history. I have carried myself as a loner, and you have all treated me as such."

"Who are you again?" said one of the other boys.

"I am your brother," I said. "We are brothers."

"My brother lives in an orphanage in the village," said the same boy. "You're just a fat kid I've never met."

"Listen," I commanded.

Anders was trying to say something, but the words were not traveling the length of the hall. I tried to hurry.

"We are in danger," I told them.

"Tell me something we don't know," said a boy who'd set up a pallet on the floor of the hall and was not getting up.

"Don't listen to him," said Nick, emerging from his room. The stings on his face and arms were still bleeding. "His stomach is full of our food and his mouth is full of his own lies." He dabbed his face with the rag he had in his hand.

"Hours ago," I said, "the Headmaster instructed me to tell you all that we were headed into a lockdown."

A collective groan.

"He was to remain in his office," I said. "But now he isn't answering the door, and my fear is that something has happened to him, or is about to happen to us."

I held up my hands to show I meant them no harm, but they did not stop eyeing me with suspicion. I had to accept the fact that they might never fully trust me, which did not mean we couldn't work together. As soon as I accepted their suspicion as one of the terms of our arrangement, it might become possible for them to actually hear what I was saying and act according to my suggestion. Whereas if I battled their suspicion, I would never reach them. I would only reinforce the necessity of their lesser instincts.

I knelt before them. "Something terrible is happening," I said.

"He doesn't have any stings at all," said the boy whose glasses would not stay on his face, stepping into the hall from Nick's room.

"I was lucky," I said.

Nick went as pale as Anders, who was still making his slow way down the hall, mumbling. He seemed lost, as if his memory had been wiped clean.

"It's the ghost," said Nick.

"No," I said.

"He's killed Hannan," said Anders, finally audible. "I've just found him."

"I only killed Thomas," I said.

Now the other boys were listening.

They tied me to a chair so I could not hurt anyone else. The knots were poor, of course, and I could have pulled my arms loose without much trouble, but my plan at this point was to deescalate things between me and the other boys, not to escape. It was important that we all get on the same page, and it was clear they needed to take this simple action against me to regain their sense of security and control.

The boys were pouring out of their rooms now. The hall was crowded with little faces, some rubbing their eyes, some quizzically taking in the scene, some excited by the sight of me bound and submissive without fully understanding the reasons behind it.

"All is not lost," I told them. "If we act as a group, nothing can overwhelm us."

"We should put him back in the gazebo," said Nick. "Let

the wasps have a fair go at him before we do anything else."
He dabbed his face, as I'd imagined he would.

"We should put him in the lake and be done with him,"
said Anders. "Hannan could never have hurt anyone. He was
a pacifist. He collected string."

"I had nothing to do with what happened to Hannan," I
said.

"We second the lake idea," said the twins.

"Why should we believe you?" said Anders.

"You don't have to," I said, "for it to be true. I am not
asking you to trust me. I am asking that we act as one. That
we work together. Which we can't do if you put me in the
lake."

"What would you have us do," said the boy whose glasses
would not stay on, "as one?"

"There are two possibilities for what is happening to us,"
I explained. "But whatever the situation is, we can only over-
come it together. We have to put all our cards on the table and
begin to play our hand as a team. As a family."

Someone in the hall blew his nose.

"Explain your theories," said Nick.

"For whatever reason, a group of us has done considerable
wrong, and we have found ourselves in a difficult position,"
I said. "But having done wrong doesn't change the fact that
we are brothers, that our situation here is unique. If we band
together, we will grow stronger than the force of our mistakes,
or any other force out there acting upon us."

"We understand that part," said a voice. "You want us to
join together. Now get on with it."

"For days now," I said, "I have been trying to wrap my

head around the situation as it has presented itself, and I have come up with two theories, as I said. First: The Headmaster, I fear, is a murderer. I found the corpse of Ms. Klein in the garden, where Thomas had his accident."

Someone in the hall snorted.

"Where Thomas fell," I said. "Later, I discovered Hannan in my closet. Dead, but not by my hand. Then I was assaulted by three boys I haven't seen since. And Fry is still missing."

"Jesus," said one boy.

"Get to the point," said another.

"Thomas?" said the boy whose glasses would not stay on.

"There is a murderous force working its way through our ranks," I said. "If it is the Headmaster, he is staging an elaborate plot to ensure someone else takes the fall. And I believe some of us, though I will not say who as I am not entirely sure, have been working with him. Now, I don't blame those who have done so. I understand you were only trying to bring things back to normal. You were only trying to protect yourself and the ones you care about here at the facility. It's an understandable position to take. I am here to say, though, that you do not have to serve a murderous Headmaster in order to ensure your survival. As one, we can restore the safety of the group. We can take back the power the Headmaster has made us believe he holds."

"What's the other theory?" said a boy whose face I could not see from my chair.

"It's something I never wanted to think, that I wouldn't let myself believe," I said. "But when I pounded on the Headmaster's door and got no answer, I couldn't shake the feeling that something terrible had happened to him. I was interrupted in my attempt to establish that he was still alive, perhaps in hiding, which would confirm the first theory, that the blame was still squarely with him. If, however, my fears are confirmed by opening that door, instead of my suspicions, then it is possible that the murderous force is here among us. It's possible it wasn't the Headmaster at all but a handful of devilish boys, who, either by accident or as malicious acts of rebellion, are responsible for the death of that man, as well as several members of our cohort and one innocent teacher."

"Ms. Klein?" said the boy whose glasses would not stay on.

"I say," I said, "that the storm is a blessing. Here to wash away our wrongdoings and let us start anew. A facility like this is a powder keg. We are provided the bare minimum in life and expected to act in a civilized and synchronous manner at all times. A single boy on his own is like a firework, endlessly crackling. A handful of boys bound together is a stick of TNT. We are explosively forceful, and they were fools to think we could be contained. It's only natural that if they put pressure on us, we would pop. It was unavoidable. Which of us can truly be blamed for what we've done so far? None. What choices did we have? Very few. But we aren't trapped by the past. We can change our behavior. We can alter our relationships and claim the results. Look to the wasps. Home is where you make it. We have lived on the street. We have lived in boarding houses and other orphanages. We've known a variety of pillows. We have been victims of circumstance from birth until this very day. But together, working as one, we can take back our lives and decide for ourselves what our home will look like. What we don't have to do is sit around here and wait for the worst to come. Something is in the air, brothers.

Something is on its way. Will we get our hands around it, or will we let it overtake us?"

"Lift him up," said Anders.

The boys surrounded me, lifting the chair from the floor.

They carried me down the hall and through the courtyard, into the facility's main building, where the Headmaster's office sat locked. They set me across from the door and went to work on it. Together, they were a battering ram. A tidal wave. A moon dislocating the oceans of the world. The Headmaster's door came apart in splinters and the boys poured through like smoke.

The window behind the Headmaster's desk was cracked open and the many pages of paper in his office were caught in a whirl of wind at the room's center. They curved toward the ceiling then fell to the floor, curling each time over the Headmaster's shoulders and horrified face, which was frozen where he sat in his rolling chair. Across from him, the fire in the fireplace roared, snatching pages every so often from the air.

"Oh no," said the boys.

Blood tapped the carpet, dripping from the Headmaster's opened wrists, and his chair was still turning, creaking as it did.

One of the twins plucked a sheet of paper from the air.

"It's Ms. Klein," he said.

"They were involved," I yelled from the hall. "Romantically."

"She's naked," said the other twin.

"Let me see," said the boy whose glasses would not stay put.

"I didn't draw them," I yelled. "I was only blamed. Please come out so we can talk about this."

"I can confirm it," said Nick. "These ones are good. His drawings are awful."

"Get them out of my face," said Anders.

I was carried to the dining hall after that. Anders fetched the remaining stragglers from the dormitory, some of whom had been sleeping peacefully, ignorant to the horrors of our situation. I watched them rub the sleep from their eyes, envious at first of those few peaceful moments they'd had, and then decidedly happy to be as I was. Unlike them, I knew what there was to know. Regardless of how this next scene would unfold, I was aware of our situation and I could fittingly absorb any new information. The other boys, still pulling themselves from whatever emotional state their dreams had rendered, would be playing catch-up for the next few hours or even days, and possibly to their demise.

There was a nervous, feverish air to the proceedings. Something seemed to have been tacitly decided by a select group, and I had to admit I was only vaguely aware of what that decision was. But it was clear that what had once been about unity was quickly looping back to a simple matter of survival.

"May I be untied?" I said, marveling to myself at how close the two words were to one another, how easily one became the next. "I'm not sure the ropes are necessary anymore."

"Quiet," said Anders, "or we'll gag you too."

They'd hauled the Headmaster's corpse onto one of the long tables near the center of the room. Boys brought candles from the dormitory and climbed on to the tables to set them in the ceramic light fixtures that hung from the ceiling. Those fixtures, punctured with an awl or needle prior to baking, cast perfect dots along the tall windows at either side of the dining hall, like stars against the howling black night. When the lightning came, it only erased them for a moment.

The boys each registered the sight of the Headmaster in different ways. Weeping, grinning, vocal disbelief, simple and silent surprise; I felt I could see all of humanity in that progression of faces. I wept too, and for all to see, as I was unable to clear my face due to my hempen strictures.

"You're right to beg," said a voice. One of the twins had found his way behind me and was tightening the ropes, which had continued to slip from the moment they'd been tied. "But it will do you no good."

"Anders," asked a small boy, of whom I had no memory whatsoever, "what's happened?"

I ignored the twin, watching instead as Anders moved past the small boy and leaned against the head of the table on which they'd set the Headmaster, looking down over the dead man's face. Something had changed in Anders's expression. He had always worn a nasty kind of scowl, but it was as if it had all been hastily wiped away, leaving only the faintest traces of the boy he once was. There was a new neutrality to his look that chilled me to the core.

"Wait until everyone has arrived," he said, looking up. "We're only going to explain it all once."

Those words, calming as they might have been on their own, were delivered in a voice that only nightmares could do justice. It was as if Anders had been wrapped in shadow or drowned in the darkness of the lake down the hill. Watching him, I felt a fear that had lived in the back of my mind for as long as I could remember move suddenly to its front. Though I had never trusted him, I'd never felt compelled to watch him closely until now. Something of significance was about to be revealed, and I understood that Anders, perhaps unknowingly, would be the one to reveal it.

He rose and moved to the door, and it occurred to me that whoever had pushed me that early night, after the fire department left us, had to have been roughly my size or larger, as he'd pushed me so effectively and confidently to the ground. And Anders was the only boy in the room who fit the bill. I was large, the largest of us all, it was true, but Anders was tall and strong. He had mean-looking arms, like two gargoyles set to protect his dull torso. It was hard to believe he actually belonged in a facility for boys. I could easily picture him drowning a grown man behind the local pub over an apple or a bit of bread.

"Is that the last of you?" he said, shutting the braided wooden door behind two small boys who walked side by side as they entered, taking each other's hands upon seeing the Headmaster splayed out on the table.

"Y-yes," said one of them. "I think so. What's happened?"

"Something terrible," said Anders, setting his fingers to their shoulders, "but also something very important."

"Klot," I said, scanning the room for any boy who might volunteer a relationship to that name. "Where is Klot?" I said, to no one in particular.

Though many of the boys stirred, their expressions revealed only fear, confusion, annoyance, or sadness. I was satisfied to see nothing that I could use, until I realized it was what I wasn't seeing that would prove useful.

Anders had not so much as looked my way when I spoke, even to determine where the noise was coming from, thereby signaling, in this critical evasion, that he and Klot, who was surely soon to appear, were co-conspirators. Anders had avoided me almost entirely since we'd entered the dining hall, and his indifference in response to my mention of Klot had been too seamless to ignore. Even when Anders spoke to me, he spoke around me, as if to look me in the eye would reignite his humanity and cause him to question all that he'd prepared. Ms. Klein, Hannan, and now the Headmaster: It had all started with Anders. Why hadn't he wanted to look at the drawings of Ms. Klein, if it weren't for his being in love with her? He wasn't religious. No orphan could ever truly believe in God. He wasn't a moral boy, as he'd made clear with all he'd done to me that evening, and in transporting and displaying the corpse of our only father figure, like a head on a pike.

I hadn't been able to see Anders clearly from the beginning, so clouded was my judgment with images of the Headmaster, who, it was now obvious to me, had only ever acted to protect me, had only ever had my interests in mind, my well-being, however inconvenient, as the foundation of his thoughts and actions. He had come to me in confidence, he had reached out to me in private, he had all but held my hand and said the words "It is going to be okay." And I had repaid him with suspicion and duplicity. I was ashamed of myself. I was disappointed in my abilities as a thinker and as a developing young man.

I watched Anders step away from the table on which they'd set the Headmaster and open his arms to the crowd. I shuddered as he began to speak.

"Boys," he said. "Thank you all for coming. I know it is late, and I know many of you had only just made it to sleep because of the storm. You'll thank me, however, when this meeting has come to its end. I should tell you all first what the new boy failed to tell us all earlier: We are locked down. By order of the Headmaster, who has always served us well, the school and its approaching roads are sealed off until the storm abates."

The room groaned and murmured, while the storm howled, rattling the loose glass in its panes. I struggled quietly against the ropes. The twin's new knots were painfully lodged against the rounded bones in my wrists, and I could feel them beginning to bruise. The whole evening had taken a dark turn, and I feared for the worst.

"We're stuck here for now," said Anders, "but we're stuck here together."

"Will we only ever make speeches and never act, except against me?" I said. "People are dead. We have to come together."

Anders nodded, as if agreeing with me in everything I'd thought and said up until that moment, but then the same twin from before gripped me by the hair and tipped back my head. When I attempted to shout in complaint, he filled my mouth with wadded fabric. It was horrid and sweet to taste, and I realized as he stepped past me, now nude from the waist up, that I was gagged with the top half of his uniform.

"No doubt some of you have heard the stories this one has been telling," Anders said, gesturing at me. "And it's possible some of you believed them. That the Headmaster had murdered Ms. Klein. That the Headmaster was staging an elaborate framing to foist the crime off on our newest addition with the limp and the baggy pants. No doubt some of you hoped this was true. You'd sensed some scandal in our midst or needed an explanation for why the Headmaster had been particularly harsh in disciplining you one afternoon. How convenient it would be for you if true. As counterargument, I present the corpse of our fine Headmaster. The body of the man who was supposedly behind the chaos that ended Ms. Klein's life and that of our beloved Hannan."

The boys murmured and writhed. They were like a cave full of snakes in a coil.

"Yes, the body count is at an alarming high," said Anders. "Hannan, Ms. Klein, Thomas—it's true, there's no doubt in that—and now our beloved Headmaster. It seems, yet again, that we have made a mistake."

The boys in the room were rapt. I couldn't believe that someone so obviously malicious and cruel in spirit as Anders was able to draw in these boys and hold them. I felt miserable watching them become absorbed in his deceit, and I realized that this was the very essence of innocence: a willingness to believe. And why every story about innocence ends with its being lost.

"We are one shy of our annual five, boys," said Anders, "and I understand the fear you all must be feeling. But I ask you not to act out of fear. Not to make any rash decisions. I ask only that you hear our case and make your decision based on the evidence, as well as any instinctively uncanny feelings you might experience in the presence of this individual, bound and gagged for your benefit."

At that moment, the doors opened to reveal a figure cast in shadow.

"Ah," said Anders. "Here we are."

"It's Fry," said one of the boys, and they all soon joined him in acknowledging the boy now entering the room.

"Fry," they said.

"Fry," they whispered.

"It's him," they said.

And it was young Fry, the boy who had served me my first sample of the full-spread nastiness that would eventually come my way at the facility, strolling through the braided wooden doors that connected the dining hall to the rest of the world, as if the recess bell had just been rung and he was reluctantly but diligently filing toward his evening chores.

He positioned himself at the front of the room, taking his time to allow us to adjust to his presence. This wasn't his first public address.

"Thank you, Anders. I can take it from here," he said. "Hello, dear friends. Have you missed me?"

I felt unexpected relief at seeing Fry alive and well. That he had color in his cheeks. That he looked well fed. He hadn't been hiding in a ditch somewhere, and he certainly wasn't buried in the garden. Still, it was obvious from the way he and Anders were presenting themselves, and from the fact that no one had removed the shirt from my mouth, that their intentions toward me weren't at all good. I tongued the shirt, trying slowly to unlock it from the hinge of my jaw. I had no plan for what I would say once the gag was removed, but it was a clear first step toward freedom, so I would take it.

"Nearly every year," said Fry, "we've believed ourselves to have found the answer. And every year so far, we've failed in some way. But can we really be blamed for that? We aren't detectives. We aren't ghost hunters. We aren't even very good at math."

The boys laughed then, settling cross-legged on the floor, as if we were going to be there for some time. Anders shook his head with affection and admiration.

It was no wonder I hadn't fit in. No wonder the boys had hardly even introduced themselves. I'd been blaming myself for my inability to get through to them, but it was also true that no one had reached out or made himself available. I had assumed this was the way of life in the facility, that it required an edgeless attitude of indifferent getting-on. And I'd been happy to go along with it. But now I understood it was only hostility not yet expressed. Those at the top, like Fry, like Anders, had been coordinating their attack, while the rest were biding their time. This wasn't a facility for orphan boys at all but an illicit hideaway for some secret society of miniature manipulators. These weren't clueless boys in the least—they were mature human beings with agendas and ideas, with the power to take a bad thought and force it to its brutal conclusion. I struggled against the ropes and licked at the gag with the root of my tongue.

"It is with great sadness that I watched our brothers fall this year," said Fry. "Great sadness and a heavy heart. But also shame. I am ashamed at us for going so far astray last year. Ashamed at our inability to see the truth amid the lies and misperceptions. The unrealities that we as a group forged into realities in the co-stoked fires of ignorance and rage. And grief. I think every night of poor Klausen's fate, and I wonder sometimes if we had any of our facts straight at all. I don't blame Thomas or Hannan for what they say they saw last year. I only blame myself for being unable to see anything else."

He paused, but purely for effect.

"This year, as some of you already know, I took it upon myself to be the watcher. Faced with the suspicion that our previous actions had not fully resolved our problem, I put it to myself to collect the evidence needed to confirm a new theory. A simple theory that, perhaps, we'd been wrong in our belief that Klausen was our ghost. Pale, strange Klausen, with his taste for murdering small animals. He wasn't our friend, but did he deserve what we did to him? Who can say, at this point? Certainly he accepted his fate. He didn't fight us. Which made it easier to believe. And I do wonder if we didn't, in fact, though incidentally, grant peace to an unrelatedly guilty conscience. What troubles might have haunted Klausen we will now never know. And though it wasn't the end of our particular mission, that doesn't mean our mistake was without positive results."

He pinched the bridge of his nose like an old scholar, and I trembled at his theatrics. The care in his delivery, the light in his eyes: I understood finally that Fry was the missing piece, not Anders. Fry had put it all in motion, and he was now carefully, confidently presenting his case against me. Anders had stayed visible, at the forefront of the action, so that he and Fry, who was working behind the scenes, could corral me toward this final showdown in the dining hall, where the rest of the group would be collectively turned against me. It was all so remarkably clever. I admired them both in that moment for what they had been able to accomplish together. Had they truly murdered everyone? Or, I wondered, perhaps more generously, had they caught wind of the murders, incorrectly blamed me, as I had incorrectly blamed the Headmaster, and as a result gone to work to guarantee I would receive justice for all they assumed I'd done? I knew I deserved to be punished for what became of poor Thomas, but I feared they misunderstood the extent of my crimes. And while I wasn't without blame, the same now seemed true of everyone in the room.

But there was hope. I refused to believe that the Klausen whose hands I'd felt in the hallway only a short while ago had been anything less or more than a living, breathing, malicious young boy, which meant that those seeking to punish him had failed in whatever terrible justice they'd tried to inflict. It followed that they might fail in their attempt to bring me to that same terrible justice, or even that Klausen was still out there somewhere, hiding and waiting for his revenge, and, upon hearing me or seeing me being dragged into the dining hall to face his same fate, could have had a change of heart and been moved to intervene, inspired by the echo of our parallel situations. Which would mean my salvation was nearly at hand. It was possible. But how likely? Could I count on one of three hellions who had locked me in a closet to come to my aid? Or would I be on my own in my final moments, forced to fend for myself?

I was sad for the other boys then, imagining myself breaking free of them and the harm I might have to inflict in doing so. They weren't wrong in seeking to put an end to the brutal suffering that ran rampant in our facility. They weren't wrong in banding together to work against a problem that affected them all. There was something admirable in their efforts. It was, in fact, what I had been after all evening, only I had been foolish enough to think that I was the first to have dreamed of it, or the only one who could achieve it. I had imagined myself leading the charge of unity, even preached that charge to a group that had, in fact, as they were demonstrating now, unified long before it had occurred to me to unify them. And they had done so, it seemed, in opposition to me. At least this semester.

"On their own, perhaps only a few of the following instances warrant consideration," said Fry, "but together they are too striking to remain unexamined. On our first day of class, I pricked our newest member with the razor-sharp end of my pencil sharpener. I'd stayed up late the night before honing its dull blade to a whisper, and yet, though I stabbed him fully and directly, not a drop of blood exited the wound. He did react in pain, but none of that life-giving formula presented itself. It wasn't enough to damn him, but it was enough to make me suspicious.

"I complained that night of an unsourceable pain and nervous evacuations, earning me an irregularly monitored bed in the medical suite, which would then become my base of operations. The following day, I began to shadow our fat, gagged friend here, and it became clear to me that, as many of you will likely have noticed, he has more than a few social problems. He has some trouble with names and faces. He lacks social grace, has trouble being polite, insists on his own way or no way at all. He is stubborn. Cruel. Self-centered. The makings of a poor party guest, indeed, but also qualities not so uncommonly associated with ghosts who fixedly haunt." He stamped his foot for emphasis.

I noticed that Nick was watching me as Fry spoke. His gaze was fearful and focused, locked into mine. I could tell he was already convinced by Fry's words, believing now that I had been the ghost all along, and I was sad to see Nick so easily swayed. So desperate to believe. I imagined his parents looking down on him from a white cloud up on high, weeping with disappointment. Nick was not going to have an easy life.

"As my suspicions came more sharply into focus," said Fry, "I was forced, over and over again, to escalate my illness for the sake of further observation, so much so that the Headmaster had doctors visiting the medical ward, professional doctors with stethoscopes and large black bags, which the Headmaster reminded me time and again the facility could not afford. And yet, he still held my hand as they administered their shots. He followed up daily to confirm I was not in danger. You know who would never have done that? Our plump prisoner here, who is only delighted right now, I'm sure, to have this much attention directed at him. When I could, I continued to shadow the baggy-trousered specter as he haunted the edges of your play and social hours, as he drew violent images of each of you being torn apart by one another, exploding at the tips of pencil sharpeners like gray balloon animals. Until, finally, he was called into the Headmaster's office to account for the images I've heard you later discovered on your own, alongside that same man's murdered corpse. These images of Ms. Klein, our first clue toward understanding the bloody proceedings that had already started to unfold, were presented to our newest nugget and he accepted responsibility for them without pause. He proudly declared himself the artist, though the quality of his other drawings might suggest this claim was a fabrication. But why? Why position himself as the artist? There's yet more to know and, in knowing, you will understand that accepting the blame for these drawings was only one of many steps in a malevolent plan, the results of which were already and would continue to be far more appalling than a few simple hand-drawn images, which the Headmaster was only looking for an excuse to forget about. For you see, gentlemen, the true nightmare was already under way, and these drawings were a mere distraction. And after what I am prepared to share with you, with my undeniable observations as evidence, we might together take the necessary steps toward what I hope will be our final solution."

The boys were rocking now, in and out of sync, like blades of grass.

"That same afternoon, this plump punisher had been assigned garden duty with poor Thomas. Our loving, sweet Thomas, who was always taking the fall for our more complicated pranks, absorbing what might have been several terrible punishments into a single compounded punishment, which he always endured without complaint. Poor Thomas, who had never even met his biological parents, who had only just arrived at the end of the year before last but had quickly and cordially made inroads with each of us, helping us when we needed help, listening when we needed to be heard. This bound bully before us led Thomas down to the garden, where they promptly unearthed the corpse of our attentive schoolteacher, Ms. Klein. With what silent pleasure did this haunt reveal the corpse to Thomas and, so quickly after this dreadful magic trick, with what direct and unhesitant malice did he attack poor Thomas, hitting him square in the face and sending him down onto the blade of a facility garden hoe.

Now, I assure you, from where I stood watching, the act appeared not only calculated but celebrated, as the boy stood over the two corpses, bouncing from one foot to the other, then lining them up, the bodies of our loved ones, laid out in the garden—the macabre yield of this year's harvest. And yet, I still couldn't be sure, not one hundred percent sure, that I hadn't simply witnessed a brutally timed accident: a misstep on behalf of a bumbling ball of butter. In over his head, no doubt, but not necessarily murderous, and certainly not yet demonstrably supernatural. And how preferable it would be to realize it was all a terrible misunderstanding. What relief I would have felt at any explanation for what I had witnessed, other than its having been the sick revels of someone bent on stamping out the peace of our small facility with his horrible, haunting heel."

The alliteration! The sheer histrionics! If I could have swallowed the gag crammed in my jaw, I might have. I couldn't stand to see Fry going on in this way, presenting such an elaborately twisted case, warping the details and casting everything in the most negative of imaginable lights. I would have been in awe of his talents if they weren't so naggingly superficial, meant only to impress our cohort and draw them into an elaborate lie that made him out to be the hero and me somehow the villain. He was a carnival barker. A trained seal. A beat poet. He was all style, and whatever substance there was to be found in his presentation was misguided and sick, meant only to subvert the humanity of these poor children and turn them over to his line of thinking. I watched him, trying to understand whether these thoughts were truly his own or if he was setting up the next nest of traps into which we all might unknowingly wander. Was this part of a grand scheme, the edges of which had not yet come into focus? Or was Fry simply trying to do what was right? To punish the one he perceived as the source of their collective danger? The only way to know was to hear him out and parse the tale he had to tell, however unbearable it was for me to have to listen to him speak.

Fry raised the edge of his hand to his forehead. "I won't go into what I saw next, boys. I will tell you the information, but I can't describe the gruesome goings-on in detail. It is too much. I lived through it once, and that was more than enough for me. There is no reason the lot of you should be forced to picture it in your minds. But, for the sake of being thorough, I will relate the broad strokes. With a cold precision that chilled me to the bone, our prisoner lifted the bodies of Ms. Klein and poor Thomas into the facility's own wheelbarrow, provided for him to transport whatever edible crops were found in the garden back to the facility for lunch the next day. He then wheeled that grisly barrow, with unearthly strength, down the hill and to the lake, where he anchored the bodies with a rock and set them in the deepest parts of the water."

A gasp traveled the room.

I shook my head at my misfortune, letting frustrated tears fall to gather in the gag.

"And then, boys," said Fry, "he came straight back to the school, into the Headmaster's office. I wondered if it wasn't to confess his crimes, so urgently had he returned, but he soon emerged with frightening focus, heading straight to his room where, through his own window, I watched him draw additional nude images of Ms. Klein. Why? I can't begin to imagine. Our minds are not one and the same. But it was obviously sinister. You could see it in the way his tongue held in the corner of his mouth, jutting out like a pink cigar. As the storm grew, I wasn't able to shadow him as effectively, and I lost him for some time following his departure from his room with the pictures. I wandered in the rain, trying to stay out of both the Headmaster's sight and the sight of the boy who, it was clear to me now, was at least a murderer, if not something far darker. And yet, of that I still could not be certain. That he is relatively new and none of us know his history, that he has trouble remembering us, that he so calmly murdered two of ours: These pieces came together to evidence the disturbed nature of an unpleasant individual, but, still, not necessarily our ghost."

The other boys were looking at me now. Some were squinting. Others were leaning behind the boy nearest them, watching me over a protective shoulder.

"It was by luck that I happened upon him again at the gazebo, only a few moments before he knocked a nest of wasps onto our poor brother Nick."

Nick nodded, his eyes still on me.

"I watched as our prisoner ran through the rain, not a single wasp sting to his person, and hid beneath the ivy on the far side of the yard. It was around that time that I heard a commotion coming from the dormitory and I headed inside, where I was presented with the corpse of Hannan."

"Hannan?" said a boy I did not know.

Looking more closely, though, I might have known him. I studied his face. There was something there that I did in fact recognize, but I could not tell what it was.

Fry nodded. He shook his head. He held up his hand as if to ask for a minute. It was all so disgusting.

"Yes," said Fry, finally. "Hannan is gone too. His body was discovered in the closet of this vile virgin."

I shuddered but all was not lost. The gears in my head were turning. Fry had revealed himself to me, though I could not yet express what I was already coming to understand.

"A few of the more rash among us had already left to go after the young thing we have presented to you this evening. They wouldn't find out about Hannan until after their return. Having seen the wounds Nick received, they were hungry for justice, and they sought out our new nightmare, bound him as he is now bound, and set him back in the fortress of wasps, knocking down several more nests in order to adequately administer that justice. While I couldn't condone their actions, I could observe the evidence that act revealed, which I will report now: the final stamp on a well-prepared document declaring his true nature, at least in my eyes. From his own dormitory window, the corpse of Hannan splayed out on the floor behind me, having fallen from the closet only a short while before, I watched as the wasps swarmed this young body. Instead of screaming, as any red-blooded boy would, he rose effortlessly from the ropes that bound him, brushed his adversaries from his hair and arms and back and legs, and returned to the dormitory without a single sting. Not a single sting. Not an ounce of visible fear. He rose, as the dead, we've learned, do rise, and made his way home. I ask you to look at Nick's face, the face of a living and breathing boy who has received dozens of stings in the presence of a single wasps' nest broken open on the gazebo floor. This bulletproof bastard was encircled by up to five wasps' nests, and yet here he sits, unbroken, not a single wound to his bulbous body. Add to that the absence of a scab or scar behind his ear where I directly nicked him earlier this semester. He receives no wound. He feels no pain that isn't performed for our benefit. He is no boy at all but a spirit wandering our halls, intent on dragging those unfortunate enough to be left alone with him down to the underworld, so that he might linger longer."

The other boys were nodding. If any hadn't been looking at me a moment before, their eyes were now locked on my gagged visage.

"You may recall his speech from before," said Fry, "designed to gain your trust and draw you under his influence. I am not here to ask the same. I am only here to present my case and allow you to make up your own minds. Setting aside the question of his incorporeality, we nonetheless have a murderer bound before us. And it is our charge now, alone as he has rendered us, to decide what we will do with him."

"But what's happened to the Headmaster?" said the boy I believed I recognized.

Fry nodded yet again. I feared his bobbled head might come tumbling off, so frequently was he nodding it, like a man about to collapse in the street.

"Upon hearing reports that the Headmaster was locked in his office, Anders and the others took matters into their own hands and brought down the door. They discovered there not only the corpse of our beloved Headmaster, but these pages." Fry waved his arm for effect, and Anders dumped a bag of torn pages from the Headmaster's office onto the table.

The other boys rushed over.

"Pictures of Ms. Klein!" said one.

"This says my name," said another. "Why does it say my name?"

"The boy whose glasses are ill-fitting," read the boy whose glasses would not stay on. "What are these?"

"Pictures," said Fry. "Our names. Descriptions. The desperate notes of a mind that cannot hold on to this world. A mind stuck between two realities: that of the living and that of the dead. We all know the symptoms. We understand the measures taken by these unfortunate creatures, still clinging madly, methodically, to a world that is no longer for them."

"We're all here," said another boy.

Fry nodded. I imagined his neck breaking like a stalk of celery.

"Yes," he said. "A great deal of work has gone into them."

"It's giving me chills to be in the same room with them," said another boy, dropping a page and shuffling away from the table. "Something has to be done."

"I agree," said Fry. "Something has to be done, and done soon. We're at four, gentlemen, as you already know. Annually, for as long as any of us have been aware of it, the count ends at five. If one more is due, let us make it the source of all our woes. Let us not lose yet another innocent like Hannan, like Thomas."

"Something has to be done!" said another boy.

"Seconded," said another.

"Thirded," said yet another.

"We're all in agreement then," said Nick. "And any who aren't in agreement should speak now."

The room was silent as a tomb until suddenly, with sus-piciously precise timing, the lights of the facility clicked on, filling the room with a golden glow and the warm, dull hum of electricity coursing back through its veins.

ILLUMINATION

A twin tightened the ropes that held me then wrapped a fresh braid around my gag. With their latest suspect securely bound, the other boys made a plan for what to do with me, and I worked out the truth about Fry. He was a natural bully, a force without subtlety or decency. He'd likely started small, as bullies do, and gradually, year after year, pushed himself beyond the comforts provided by discreet acts of casual violence and onto a more public stage, opening himself up to the possibility of doing true harm.

I couldn't say exactly where, when, or why it had begun; maybe there was an accident one day, a boy found at the bottom of a well, a broken neck in proximity to a tipped-over ladder, something the world would look to sweep under the rug, would thank God to have a reason to believe was an accident, something that, with enough precaution, care, and attention, could be avoided in the future. I thought of the poor Headmaster, blaming himself for some mysterious harm that had come to a child in his charge. Fry would have been emboldened by that, would have found his new extracurricular

activities too thrilling to quit, too satisfying to revert to anything less, and he would have kept them up, refining them
into bolder, more malicious, more grandiose schemes. Then,
completely immersed in his own malevolence, he might have
found himself suddenly facing a number of corpses beyond
simple explanation. Confronted with a suspiciously high body
count, he might have circulated a rumor that the halls were
haunted. Casually at first, but consistently. The Headmaster
wouldn't have believed it, but at the very least it would have
put the other boys on edge, confirming their fears, possibly
making them suspicious of one another or doubtful of their
own minds, turning any nighttime sounds into the laughter
or celebration of a malicious spirit. The possibility of a ghost
would have infected them, as it had infected Nick. Fry had
also likely made the rounds, scaring the other boys night after
night, keeping up the momentum of their mounting sense of
dread, so that they would fall quickly in line when he presented a route to safety. By giving the other boys something
to believe in, something to fear, Fry had given them something to band together against. As the orchestrator of their
shared delusion, he could easily direct the incredible force of
these boys as he pleased. Though this was technically a goal
we'd shared, a punch he'd simply beaten me to, I did not
lump myself in with Fry. His execution relied on delusion,
whereas mine relied on truth. Effective as it was, his approach
allowed me to understand the most important distinction between myself, admittedly not without guilt, and Fry, whom
I believed to be, if not evil, then the closest manifestation
this secular world could produce. Fry had taken a position of
power based on lies and manipulation, and for the purpose of

personal gain. It was true he'd provided a kind of unity, but it was a false unity, and one that ran the risk of someday forever dividing those who believed themselves to have been unified. When they discovered it wasn't actually a banding together but a being bound, how would they respond? They would turn their backs on the very idea of unity. Or they would turn to it only in the spirit of Fry. Those who were unsuccessful in taking power as he had would be destroyed by a world that resents being bent to the will of the weak. Those who were successful, few as they might be, would only further divide humanity, having the same long-term effects that Fry had had on their group and adding to the ever-expanding reach of this ultimately divisive method of unification. The cycle, I realized, could go on forever, until someone selflessly made an effort to end it.

My jaw was aching from the gag, and my wrists were raw. How many hours had we been at this? How many more were left?

"We could burn him," said one of the boys.

"No," said another. "He could survive it."

"We could put him in the lake with his corpses," said Nick.

Fry shook his head. "And leave him for future generations to surface?" he said.

"What about a cave?" said another. "We could put him in a cave in the mountains and seal it with an enormous rock."

"Boys," said Fry.

They turned.

"Why do ghosts haunt?"

"Because they're evil," said one of the many I'd once considered a brother.

"Because they are looking to right the wrongs they suffered in life," said another.

"Because something terrible happened, and they are like a bruise on the world of the living," said a third.

Fry shook his head. He stood again at the front of the room and lifted his hands.

"Brothers," he said, "forget what you've heard. These are mere metaphorical imaginings, dreamed up by those who would seek to find meaning in our nightmares. Ghosts haunt because they simply do not know any better. They haunt because they are confused. They don't know what they are, or what they are to do, and they act according only to impulse, habit, and routine. They circle the familiar places of their life, not lovingly but compulsively. Our captive will forever be a captive, either ours or at large in the world of the living, until the moment he realizes this isn't where he belongs. This isn't his home. If that doesn't happen, he will only make smaller and smaller circles, as his consciousness dims and his memories fade. And as his emotional and psychological connections to our world deteriorate, he will cling more desperately, and increasingly he will act out, with growing violence and anger. The world of the living can't be made sense of by the dead. It is that simple. It's beyond them. He needs to be shown that he is dead. That this is not his world. And then, maybe, he will cease to haunt it. He has to see that a line has been crossed before he can go back to the other side."

"How do we know he'll listen?" said the boy whose face I could not remember.

"He won't listen," said Fry.

"Then how do we explain it?" said another.

"As I've said," said Fry, "we have to show him."

"Do we have evidence of his death?" said the boy whose glasses would not stay on. "Can we hold up a mirror and make him see how dimly he flickers?"

Fry shook his head. He held up both hands to quiet the room.

"If a ghost is wounded," said Fry, "he believes he feels pain. He understands that what is happening should be painful, and it is then experienced as pain, even if his nerves are corroded. Just as, bound, he believes he cannot move."

I squirmed, and the binds abraded my wrists.

"A ghost is memory granted form," he said. "But what is missing when a ghost is wounded? What is something that cannot be produced from memory, but exclusively by the beating hearts of the living? What separates us from this hollow shell we have bound to our dining hall chair?"

"Blood," said Nick, rubbing his wrists.

Fry nodded. He looked to Nick. "Blood," he said.

"What does that mean?" said one of the smaller boys.

"We have to show him that his veins are simple shadows," said Fry. "We have to open them, spread the curtains of his forearm, and reveal the empty stage beneath."

It was really too much, the way he was carrying on, but it didn't change their horrid intentions.

"Get a knife," said Anders.

"We'll get knives," said the twins.

I screamed into the gag, and no one looked my way.

How had it come to this? Was I getting what I deserved or was I stuck in some spiraling nightmare, a surreal pageant of pseudo-rationality wherein the worst parts of our nature wore wigs of reason and sense? The twins, of course, had left for the kitchen to find the sharpest knife. Could these boys truly want what was about to happen? Did they have any idea how it would go? Had they talked themselves into it, or had they merely masked their basest desires in an attempt to blend in with those they perceived as loving and thoughtful humans? I have said it before, but I must restate it as it occurred to me in light of those recent events: Young boys are barbarians.

Each held a conversation with the person closest to him, and there was a moment, in the glow of the dining hall lights, when the sound of those voices echoed the sound that always followed our meals, when we were done eating and collectively waiting for recess to begin, when the conversations were trivial in nature and the room was swollen with the electricity of boys anticipating a flash of unbridled play. I found myself lost in that echo, feeling throughout my body the momentary comfort of anonymity and normalcy, the routine of our early days together, wherein I was nothing and no one to any of them and the only matter at hand was when recess would be called, when our legs would stretch and the room would fill with the padding of our heeled shoes, which we would pile outside the door after we'd spent thirty minutes running in the mud, tackling in the mud, screaming into the mud, as we had once loved to do, long before any corpses had been unearthed, before any devastating accidents had occurred or any dark secrets had been revealed. I could hear the twins arguing in the kitchen. I shut my eyes, anticipating the crack of the braided door as it blew open and then the crowd heading my way.

When the sound did not come, I opened my eyes. There

was shouting, followed by a scream, and a twitch worked its way around the room as each boy startled and grew silent. They looked to me to confirm that I was still bound and gagged, and then they looked in the direction of the sound from before, toward the kitchen, wherein the twins had surely been testing the knives in some gruesome fashion.

The first twin burst through the braided door with only the time to shout, "Grab him!" before the other twin, still shirtless, entered in pursuit.

I watched with horror as the shirtless twin plunged one of the wooden-handled butcher's knives into his brother's back. That twin shrieked as I saw the glint of the knife's pointed end emerge a centimeter or so from the front of his body. The second twin removed the knife and plunged it in once more.

"Look," he yelled. "Look!"

Several boys set upon him and wrested the knife from his hand.

"Look at his wounds," shouted the stabbing twin. "Let me go!"

The other twin was covering the wounds with his hands, as if trying to catch the blood that would soon come spilling from them. The blood that had not yet come spilling, I realized, only a second or two before the other boys began to understand what was being presented. My lead on the thought did nothing for me, as I was still bound and gagged, still their prisoner, still helpless in the face of whatever was about to unfold, but I found myself feeling a sense of pride nevertheless at having gotten there first. I held my realization in my head like a pearl, knowing it had value and knowing I was without a clue as to what I might do with it.

"It's him!" someone shouted. "It's the ghost!"
"Yes," said the shirtless twin. "Grab him!"
"No, grab him!" said the first.
"Untie me!" I muffled into the gag.

The twins were grabbed and held apart by several boys each. Fry stood on the edge of the scene, alternating between watching me and watching the twins and the other boys. He had an almost disappointed look on his face, which less observant parties might have taken for concern, but which confirmed nonetheless my suspicion that it was not the truth he was after but any excuse at all to bring me harm. I could see the aggravation welling up in him as the reality of our situation announced itself to the room. His blame had been miscast. The steps he'd taken to assure the others would go along with his plan, however elaborate they'd been, did not account for this unexpected disruption. This sudden and unwelcome revelation. My salvation at the hands of two nightmares with the same face. It was eating him up.

Whether or not he was a true enemy, one set against me beyond all means of recovery, in that moment I felt that Fry embodied all I objected to most in the world. No good would ever come from him, only harm and misinformation. He was a snake, I realized, concerned only with himself and the perversion of others. I would have to be the garden hoe that chopped his head.

The garden hoe. I might have laughed if the gag weren't so strongly pitted against it. It was as if my subconscious mind operated at twice the speed of my impulses, anticipating where they would lead me, the actions I might desire to take, and had therefore oh so casually dropped a loaded object in

THE JOB OF THE WASP

my path to disrupt me. The garden hoe. I was a better person than I knew.

The last time I had taken action without thinking it through, I'd accidentally robbed poor Thomas of his life with that very implement. It couldn't have been a good life, Thomas's, but that was for him to discover through the process of living it. That is one of the great tragedies of any life, I thought, watching Fry, thinking of Thomas, that you can't know it is a tragedy until you have experienced it in full. You might anticipate its being tragic, but there is always the possibility that things will shift in your favor and go suddenly, unexpectedly your way. There is always the possibility that all the things you've ever dreamed of will wind up in your lap, either through great effort on your part or by simple chance. It is also possible, perhaps even more likely, that the tragic circumstances of a particular period in life will wear themselves out and you will find yourself with some semblance of peace among the ruins. Life consists of extremes, I told myself, screaming into the gag, so there is always the possibility that what is being experienced at any given moment is actually the worst it will ever get, and there is only room for improvement. So those with low expectations go on living, anticipating nothing but tragedy but living nonetheless, all the way up until the moment when the fullness of that tragedy is realized, when all the pieces that have been in play for years finally come together and you are faced with your great humbling. The bedrock bottom. Where, from out of the mud and muck of your life, out of the peach pit of despair that has replaced your heart, comes the impulse to die, to be done with it all, to no longer have to think of anything related to life or how you've failed yourself and all those around you. Or so it seemed to me was the case in that moment, tied to the chair and gagged while the room conspired against me. So I imagined my life would go, as would the lives of all these boys, who were wrestling now, either with the twins or with the predicament they were in, torn between the reality that the twins had now presented and the information Fry had delivered so floridly only a few moments before. Fry, however, did not seem torn. He seemed put out. A little sour and a lot exhausted. Like a boy without a prize.

The twins were being processed, and each was protesting the presentation of the other, arguing for the accuracy of their personal account of what had happened in the kitchen, but I could only watch Fry as he set himself down on one of the benches before the table on which they'd placed the Headmaster, roughly at the dead man's hands, covering his own face so the others wouldn't see his dissatisfaction at the recent sequence of events.

I am not always as strong as I would like to be. I have a great deal of will, but it is fragile. Seeing Fry there, possibly my mortal enemy but in a moment of weakness, I found that my heart did wince. I did imagine him being comforted in some way, though by a force I could not grant definition, and I can admit it was a pleasing thought. There is something that binds humans to one another, however awful we can be in our lesser moments. I don't know what it is, but I was nonetheless happy to feel something like compassion for my enemy. My heart went out to Fry in that moment, and, in that it did so, it moved me. To my unexpected satisfaction, I was reaching out to him from behind my gag and wishing him well. The energy in the room had turned yet again.

"I'll take out the gag," said one of the boys. I didn't recognize him at first, but as he approached, I realized it was the boy who had stuck his hands in my armpits to help me up after I was pushed on the night of the fire alarm. He looked tired, maybe even sick. He had black circles under his eyes, and he was wet with sweat.

I nodded. *Yes*, I thought, *please do. The gag, yes, please.*

"He'll curse us," said the twin who'd been stabbed but still wasn't bleeding.

"Enough," said Nick, who held the stabbed twin in place with the help of several other boys.

I watched that twin, who wasn't bleeding, and realized the wound itself would require examination before I could come to any real conclusions. It was dark in the dining hall, despite the light, and I was so far away. The blood might have been there after all, hidden in the shadows of his shirt or behind his palms. Or maybe he wasn't much of a bleeder? I needed a better look to understand exactly what had happened, but unfortunately no one there shared the priority.

The boy who had once lifted me from the floor did soon approach, however, untying the rope that held the gag in place. My jaw screamed with pain as it closed my mouth for the first time in what felt like hours.

"My God," I said, "that was terrible." The bone at the hinge of my jaw popped as it opened and shut.

"Are you not the ghost?" said the boy.

"No," I said. "Of course not. Remember, I was pushed in the hall. You helped me. I was bloody then."

He nodded, but I saw no recognition in his eyes.

"After the fire alarm," I said, as he stepped away.

"Wait," said the stabbed twin. "You have to understand that I am being set up. If anyone is the ghost in this room, it is my brother, who fell upon a broken lightbulb in the kitchen and came up without a scratch."

"No," said his brother. "You fell on the bulb."

"You did!" said the first twin. "Which is why I came bolting in here like I did."

"You came bolting in here because you knew I was going to tell them," said the other.

"And then he stabbed you," said Nick. "We all saw it. Yet here you are, alive and healthy enough to go casting the blame on whomever you like, including your own brother."

The stabbed twin paused for a moment. He looked to his brother. Was he smiling?

"But why did you tell them?" he said.

His brother seemed taken aback. I could already see the grief in his face. Maybe it had always been there. A well of suffering we had all mistaken for malice.

"I don't know," he said, as if he were discovering the words for the first time. "I acted without thinking."

How broken was I that I began to feel pity for these two monstrous twins as well? The most bloodthirsty of the bunch, yet their appeals to one another raised goosebumps underneath my restraints.

It was true they had angelic faces. They shared one angelic face. With the same small nose, roughly the size of a fingertip, and icy blue eyes that made you think of the sky in bright winter.

We were all emotional that night. I wasn't the only one crying.

"Brother," said his brother, as a tear fell from their shared chin, "have I left this world already?"

His brother shrugged. There were tears in his eyes as well now, or perhaps it was a trick of the light from across the room. Either way, it was obvious from the way he spoke that he was torn up.

"I don't want to go anywhere without you," said the stabbed twin.

"You won't," said his brother, accepting back his shirt, my former gag, from the boy who'd helped me.

Dressed again, that same twin turned to the crowd of boys, who were still not ready to hear it. "Open both of our veins," he said, "and let us know the full truth once and for all."

"Wait," said Nick. "Let's think this through. It can't be both of you, can it?"

Fry was still at the table, his head in his hands, and I was confident I heard him yawn.

"It's better this way," said the twin who'd done the stabbing. "If he has to go, however and wherever it is that he goes, I'll go with him."

"I won't do it," said Nick. "I get sick at the sight of blood."

"Assuming there will be blood," said the twin who was not bleeding.

"Assuming," said Nick. "Yes."

"I'll do it," said Fry, standing abruptly and knocking his knees against the table. "I brought us all here. This was my grand presentation. I was ready to do it to this one." He gestured at me without looking. "I should be man enough to do it to these two."

Already Fry was getting back on my nerves. Man enough.

How could he possibly have the stomach for all this? He'd dreamed up the ghastly punishment, inspired everyone to believe in its necessity, and now he wanted to perform the act himself, not just on one boy, but on his brother to boot. There was something horribly wrong with him, I had no doubt. It is one thing to dole out justice after it has been decided upon by the group, but it is a different thing entirely to conjure such a twisted event and then volunteer to do the carving. No, I decided, as pitiable as he might seem in certain moments, he had to go. I didn't have to feel good about it, and it didn't mean I was without guilt. But I'd thought it through enough to understand what had to be done. I could save the world a great deal of suffering. I could save myself a great deal of suffering. I could maybe even help these twins, who had disturbed me before, it was true, but who were now growing in my esteem.

Slowly, the other boys brought the twins together, and which was which faded from my mind. I knew there were differences between them, but those differences fell away, as I looked from one to the other, failing to set them apart.

Fry walked the length of the dining hall and lifted one of the knives from the brick floor.

"Are we all in agreement?" he said.

"It doesn't matter what they think," said one of the twins.

"Just do what we ask," said his brother.

"Where is all this coming from?" said Nick. "You two have always had a lust for life."

"He is my only family," said one of the twins. "And we've done everything together. I've only ever known a world with him in it, and there's nothing we haven't shared. If he's a ghost, then it stands to reason that I'm a ghost too. There's no way I would have let him die without me. And if he hasn't in fact died, if there is some other explanation for all this, I won't remain alone on this earth to discover it without him."

"Nor will I," said his brother. "Wherever we go, whatever we know, we do it together."

They clasped hands.

Nick shook his head but no longer spoke in protest.

What kind of place was this? What had I entered into? Would the communal thirst for blood be sated after the butchering of these two doppelgängers? Maybe for a semester. Possibly two, given that they were twins. But then what? Who would be next?

"May this bring you peace," said Fry.

"Wait," I said, from across the room.

He drew the blade across their wrists, one after the other, and the room held its breath.

Had the rain stopped? I hadn't heard it in what felt like hours. I watched the dark window and saw nothing.

"Oh no," said one of the twins. He had not let go of his brother.

"Now would you look at that," said the other.

Together, they raised their clasped hands and presented the skin of each, flapping like flags in the breeze. Not a drop fell, to my eye, and they were smiling.

"I wonder when it happened," said one of the twins.

"It doesn't really matter, does it?" said his brother.

They turned toward the doors then, hand in hand.

"Wait," I called.

The door did not open. They did not pass through it. They

simply vanished. The backs of their heads were replaced by the decorative braids that traced the edges of its wood. Or maybe I'd blinked as they'd stepped through a small opening, a thin crack in the nearly closed door that I couldn't make out from where I'd been placed. It was only a moment later, and I was already uncertain as to what I had seen. If I could have rubbed my eyes; if they had let me move closer.

Fry let the knife fall. Other boys clung to one another. A few sat stunned at the scattered tables. There was no thunder or lightning. Had the rain really stopped? I wondered. I couldn't hear it. I couldn't hear anything.

"Untie him," said Nick, pointing at me, finally without malice, "and let's go bury the Headmaster."

The decision was made to bury him in the garden. It was still dark out, but there were lanterns in the hallway closets of the dormitory, and we sent a group to collect them. We would bury the Headmaster and Hannan together, in the loose dirt, and maybe one day we would eat a pumpkin in their honor. It made us smile, but it was not a joke.

No one was friendly after they untied me, but they were no longer trying to kill me, which I considered progress. We didn't speak as we made our way down the hill to the garden, the Headmaster in the wheelbarrow and Hannan wrapped in a sheet, carried by several boys at each end.

We took turns digging, and I kept looking to the horizon, expecting the sun to appear one moment after the next. But it didn't. I had no sense of what our plan for the future would be. Our plan for the facility. It wasn't the right time to ask.

It all seemed to make sense to the other boys, so I let it go, taking my turn with the shovel and trying to act as agreeable as possible. It was clear to me that unity could never truly be achieved if everyone wanted to lead the unification process. I had gone about the project all wrong, storming in and demanding respect. I had expected it and accepted nothing less. It was no wonder they'd wanted to open me up.

The boy who could not keep his glasses on spoke over the graves after we were done with them.

"I have a poem to read," he said, taking a lantern and holding it up as he withdrew a bit of paper from his pocket. "I've only just written it," he said, "and it's not very good."

Each of us found some part of the earth to watch as he read.

"I am a little bug," he said. "Maybe not one of the ones that stings, but one people still bat away or crush with a book. Maybe one that people aren't afraid of, but one they don't necessarily want to look at. I once had a fold of fabric under which I was protected. To which I could comfortably cling and where I felt safe, which is important because a bug is always in danger. But it is the nature of cloth to move and unfold. It is the nature of weird little bugs to move too, though cloth is never afraid, as we bugs can be. Today I am shaken from my fold and falling. That's all I've got so far."

He was right. It wasn't good. We applauded his efforts and began our silent ascent of the hill.

In the morning, maybe some of us would go for help. Or maybe we would live out the rest of the summer alone at the facility, placing orders with the grocer and the tailor on the Headmaster's behalf. I had no sense of how the other boys would want to handle the situation. I released the notion that I should be the one figuring it out. I released the notion that it would need to be figured out at all. Since my arrival, I had been moved through a series of events with very little control over what happened from one moment to the next. I saw my mistake as that of the nervous man in quicksand. All along I had been struggling, sinking faster and wearing myself out. But here was a second chance, an opportunity to amend any errors of judgment and action. I would listen to my brothers at the facility and I would try to be calm. I would try to rest. Surely there was a sound mind among them.

I looked to the others as we moved up the hill. I hardly recognized their faces, as I hadn't taken the time to get to know them. Each was unfamiliar to me, or only recently and tenuously made familiar. It was as if I had just arrived at the facility, though I had been there for months, living with these boys whose faces I had failed to even register. I was disgusted with myself in that moment. Or disappointed. I was melancholy on our walk back up to the facility. I thought of all there is in life that goes unnoticed. All that I had failed to absorb in my self-centered and steadfast barreling. I could start living for others, I realized, when we began our new life together. Not every plan had to be one that I agreed with, or even one I understood. Not every plan had to be designed to move me forward. Those rarely panned out besides. I could celebrate and learn from the individualities of my cohort. I could do what they asked, when they asked it, and we might one day find some common humanity. One that had nothing at all to do with understanding or rationality but was based solely on service and collaboration. I didn't have to understand my brother to help him. And which of these boys could not use help?

I'd failed to see it before. I hadn't allowed myself. It was the same with the Headmaster. All he had ever done was try to help me, and I'd spent all my time trying to pick apart his every move. Wrenching every good intention into a talon. Our poor Headmaster, who had been nothing but patient, who had packed up and come to stay with us during a thunderstorm out of love and fear for our safety, who had left his wife and warm fire and steaming cup back at home and come to serve a group of boys, the newest member of which was an ungrateful paranoid, suffering from conspiratorial delusions that had left him friendless, without sympathy, and so distanced from reality as to make him hardly lament the numerous deaths he'd witnessed over a period of a few days, not to mention the one death he had actively participated in, had in fact caused. So many corpses piling up, so many severances and so much suffering, and this new boy, fat with greed and anxiety, had only thought to work out how it all related to him, how every incident seemed part of a constellation that ultimately came together to form the image of his own grubby face. Yes, a grand conspiracy directed at me. Of course that was it. How sensible and astute.

On our brief trek up the hill, I couldn't understand how I had been so stupid and yet felt so smart. It was astonishing to think of how right I could feel while being so incredibly wrong. In my mind, every piece had fit together, whether or not I'd had to force it. Of course it was all an overly complicated plot to cover up the murder of our beloved Ms. Klein, rather than a twist in the natural chaos of living, a simple, tragic expression of the one wholesale truth of our corporeal existence, that it one day, comically, accidentally, suddenly, horrifically, comes to an end. A truth that had nothing at all to do with me or my life in the facility. Confronted with the unexpected death of Ms. Klein, the Headmaster had perhaps meant to respond quietly and privately, out of kindness, so that he might spare those of us in our youth more grief. It had simply been an accident, my discovering her body in the garden. I'd had nothing to do with it at all until I inserted myself.

I felt a deep connection with those now dead, as none of us had ended up where we'd expected. That connection then extended to the other boys as well, who were alive and swarming around me on our way up the hill, like wasps knocked from their nest. We were starting over. Working back toward some semblance of normalcy yet again. Only this time, I would meet them in the swarm. I would join the others, and our life together would unfold as it saw fit. And, armored as we now were by our shared experience of the recent and life-altering events at the facility, we could more easily face the undeniable challenges of any human life head-on. As we each inevitably fell away in the years to come—as humans have always done and will always do—we might say our final farewells in whatever fashion we preferred, nodding or waving or smiling or wailing as our strange family, one by one, vanished through a braided door. I imagined myself on my back in bed, some day in the distant future, and a much older Nick rushing to my side to tell me that one of the other boys was approaching his end. The group of us would gather around that sick boy's bed, intermittently holding his hand or his arm, telling jokes and stories about our early years together, until he was gone. It was beautiful to imagine, however far away it felt.

Moved as I was by the thought of Nick one day rushing to my side, I also felt a twitch of something in the back of my mind that would not yet present itself in full, so successfully had I surrendered to the spirit of the group. I climbed on, up the hill, but the itch did not pass, so I made one last effort to focus on the idea, to see what was there and to understand its relationship to the comforting thoughts I'd only just been having. One last effort to think through whatever was bubbling up in the back of my brain so that I might release it, as I had done with all my other impulses toward heroics.

And, after a moment, it came to me, just as the storm had set on, or as the wasps had lifted from their nest when it split, that the Headmaster's wife was still at home, anticipating her husband's return. There was no knowing at this point how long it had been since he left. How many days she imagined he would be sleeping at the facility with us. She would have been pacing around the house that night, ignorant to his new resting place in the garden and to the situation of his heart. It grieved me to think of it. I couldn't have spoken if someone had asked me to in that moment, so choked was I then by the image of his dog, coiled in the seat his master usually occupied, grateful in that rare comfort for the Headmaster's absence but also eager for his rapid return. What kind of woman was she? I wondered. Was she made anxious by the storm? Probably not, if he'd been so willing to depart during the crisis of it. I imagined she was fairly independent. Our Headmaster was too soft around the waist and kind in the eye to have married someone who needed a ballast. On the contrary, I imagined she'd supported him in times of emotional strife. As Nick would one day rush to my side, I understood that one of us must now rush to hers. It would be too cruel to just leave her as she was: home, alone, no doubt enjoying the peace but still eagerly anticipating the return of a loved one. Her only family. Her doting husband. And how he must have doted on her! Our kind and beloved Headmaster.

Once again, I was confronted with the need to take action. While I wanted desperately to drift into the background of our new life together at the facility, I could never truly give myself over to it now, not with the thought of the Headmaster's wife still scraping at the back of my skull. Every moment that passed without her knowing the truth added to her inevitable suffering. To realize that we had known and not told her. That we'd buried her husband without her, said our goodbyes without her, then moved on, back toward a new life on the hill, without saying a word. It was too much to bear. I would go down immediately, and I would tell her outright what had happened. I would do my best to console her in the face of her new tragic situation, and then I could rejoin my brothers at the facility. I could ease into the background after that—as I had already started to do, and as I so longed to do—and allow things to come as they may.

I dropped my pace and let the slower boys move around me. It wasn't a complicated plan, and it wouldn't take long, just a single conversation on the subject, along with whatever explanations she might need plus however many repetitions she might request when it came to the stranger details. In her distant way, the Headmaster's wife was still a part of our family there at the facility, and I would be providing her a necessary

156

service, however difficult it would be, just as I'd been celebrating the importance of doing only moments before.

I watched the other boys drift slowly homeward, certain it was better in all respects not to alert them of my departure. Why burden them with this final grim task? Why force them to confront the thoughts I was now having, of the Headmaster's wife wrapped in an enormous green shawl, huddled by the fire and glancing up every so often to view a picture of our deceased Headmaster, radiant with love for him, grateful to have him in her life, though maybe they did not always get along, it was true, but still he was hers and she was his, and their life together must have been fairly good, as far as lives went. Why add to the night's collective suffering? How much could these boys take? And why run the risk of a debate? No. I would slip away without their noticing, as I'd done so many times before, and head down the hill to her small home. I would tell her on my own. Then we would be done with it. Then I would be done. I could tell the boys after, and they would be grateful to have it over with. Grateful even to me, maybe, for having taken it on myself. The last thing the new widow needed was twenty-five or so boys showing up at her door in the middle of the night, scrambling to tell her that two of their cohort had possibly murdered her husband then vanished through the braided wooden door of our dining hall. That wouldn't do. Alone, I could be casual in my presentation but sympathetic. I could focus on her and her loss, and make room for her suffering. I would hardly be there at all. I had never done anything like it before, but I was fully confident in my ability to perform this final task as it needed to be done.

THE WIDOW AND DEATH

The walk down to the Headmaster's home was a solemn one. I first had to pass back by the garden, where the dirt was freshly turned, and by extension the lake, which sat like an abyss on the horizon. The earth was wet with rain. Branches and leaves were scattered over the hill and in the grass. Everything was still, as it tends to be after a storm, but somehow radiant, as if the lightning had left in all of it some small bit of its charge. I could not remember the last time I'd wandered outside after a storm, so I took in the scene as if it were my final opportunity.

Above me there were no stars granting definition to the infinite mass that envelops us. I thought for a moment of our insignificance, then cast aside the idea. If we were truly insignificant, then there was nothing more trivial than pondering insignificance. There were bodies in the garden, in the lake, and I had been saved by a brother, who had, in order to do so, sacrificed not only his own family but himself. Insignificance seemed hardly to matter at all.

I imagined myself collapsing on the hill and letting the

sun rise up around me, warming the dew from my body and blocking out the starless dark. Yes, I was cultivating poetic impulses. I was in search of an elegant phrase or thought. I wanted to somehow acknowledge this occasion, my final solitary excursion before I returned to the facility of orphaned boys, and a celebration of my life thus far. Our lives thus far. It was remarkable to me, and so I searched for my remarks.

I spotted smoke in the distance, and then the dark roof of the Headmaster's home. The lake was just out of view now, which was lucky for me, I realized, though unlucky, I felt, for the Headmaster and his wife. Still, when I finally set my eyes on it, their home seemed like the best any of us could hope for in this life, view or no. It was a small house on a green hill, privately owned, with smoke leaving the chimney and no one banging at the door. It was theirs, their small part of the world, like a burrow carved directly into the earth by hand, and the two of them had lived there in accordance with their hearts, quietly making do for as long as they could.

I'm not sure why I felt so confident the conversation would go well. For days, my actions and encounters had led only to more distress, more danger. Nothing I'd attempted turned out as I intended. Even so, I was pleased to find myself nonetheless compelled toward a final act of kindness before falling in with my brothers at the facility. Simply having made it down the hill without question or trouble brought to boil in me an inexplicable self-assurance that refused to cool no matter what worry I blew its way.

When I arrived, I raised the knocker and let it fall. Their walkway was made of large stones lined up like lily pads. A metal vase full of flowers had been tipped off the porch by the rain, and I was bending to set it right as the black door groaned open.

"Ashley," said an old woman in an enormous green shawl. Her eyes were nearly white, as if a tablecloth had been placed over them, but I could still see their former blue beneath the transfiguration of old age, as well as the quick movements they made when she examined me.

"No," I said, "I'm sorry. I'm new to the facility. Or relatively new, and I've come with some delicate information. I think we should sit down inside, if you have a set of chairs we might be able to use."

"It's very late," she said.

There was something labored in the way she spoke, as if she held something in her mouth. I would have worried I'd interrupted her at dinner, but as she'd just reminded me, it was late.

"I know," I said. "I can't begin to tell you how long the night has been for me. But I've arrived with something you'll want to hear, and the sooner we get to it, the better for both of us. You'll have to trust me."

"Always so urgent, Ashley," she said. "But of course, if you want to talk, yes, let's talk."

I righted the vase, but it tipped again the moment I let go, dumping more of the flowers off the porch and into the mud. The sound of it hitting the stone at our feet echoed a sound I'd heard before but could not place.

"I'm sorry," I said.

"The flowers don't mind," she said.

She stepped aside, making room for me to move past her and into the house, which smelled so intensely of pumpkin pie I nearly vomited. It's possible I'd felt like vomiting for some time and my body had only finally found its excuse. Either way, I was still for a moment as I choked it back, and when she looked at me I was able to conjure a smile.

"What is that smell?" I said, as she signaled for me to follow her to the hearth, where two chairs sat on either side of a small fireplace, in which a low fire was burning.

"Excuse me," she said. "I'm not sure. The rain sometimes gets into the support beams under the roof, which can make the place feel like an old cave. Is that what you're smelling?"

"No," I shook my head. "I assure you it's not."

"It might be the chair you're sitting in," she said. "I can't say I remember the last time it was washed, and Henry never showers without sitting down for a few minutes in front of the fire after work. It's thick with his must, I'm sure."

Henry the Headmaster. It split me open to hear his name spoken so plainly, so unknowingly, so hopefully, almost as if it were the very first time it had been said aloud. I pushed any thoughts of pumpkin pie and vomit as far from my mind as I could. *My God, this poor woman*, I thought. Where would I even begin?

"I'm afraid I have some bad news," I said.

"Let's not start there then," she said. She settled into her chair, placing her feet on a crocheted ottoman set before it. "Some people like the bad news first. Me, I prefer to ease into it." At this point, she belched, articulating the chamber of her ribs. "I've just had some pork," she explained, her hand to her mouth.

It endeared her to me that she was so comfortable around me, and that I'd been correct in my observation that she might recently have been eating.

"Where should we start, then?" I said.

"Tell me how your semester has been," she said. "Are you excited for summer?"

"Well," I started, but I didn't know where to go from there. The impulse to spill the whole story, from start to finish, held my tongue in place. There was no other story to tell, none of consequence that occurred to me, and yet it didn't feel entirely right to launch into the raw details in our very first moment together.

In truth, I couldn't imagine a moment between us wherein it would feel entirely right to explain all that had happened. It seemed somehow wrong of me, as if I would be forcing her to endure it. Everything around us was designed to put her at ease, to bring her comfort and a sense of well-being, and I had a story that would act like a bucket of old fish, spilling into the room and ruining it for her for the foreseeable future. How could I do that to this poor elderly woman, who was now entirely on her own, with no one to care for her? I felt immense pity for her, and then, unexpectedly, for myself.

After all, this woman had had Henry the Headmaster for years. They had lived together, long and well, had made this home together, had supported and loved one another. I could tell from the minute I'd walked in: This was a loving home. And I'd never had anything of the sort, at any point in my life. No home to call my own. No relationship of any consequence. Every plan I'd made to connect with my cohort had failed. Every person who had reached out to me I'd pushed away— suspiciously, violently, cruelly, and desperately. If tonight had actually proven to be my final night on this earth, as it had seemed would be the case many times throughout, I would have died as I'd entered this world, alone and without having had any impact on it at all. It would be a death that did not register with a single living soul, other than those who might have found some comfort in bringing it to pass. I had not known the boys in the halls, and they had not known me. In a year, would any of them even be able to recall my face?

"Yes," I said. "I am excited for summer."

"Ashley," she said, "it's going to be okay, dear."

She had closed her eyes, as if we were listening to music I could not hear. The fire clicked and the house went silent. I watched her for several minutes, waiting for anything more, but she seemed content to stay that way until the morning came for us. I wondered, though only for a second, if she would actually let me sit with her through the night. I might have liked it, though it was hard to say. But for a strange moment it did feel like we were alone together on the edge of the world, and that I was somehow both vulnerable and entirely safe.

There might have been a different way to say it. A different story to tell, and one that was far less urgent. After all, it was possible no one had actually murdered the Headmaster. However unlikely it was for his death to have been entirely independent of all the other deaths, that didn't necessarily mean it was not so. And the same was true of each death, in fact. Their happening in close sequence to one another wasn't hard evidence of their being linked in any way. I wondered, finally, and after all I'd been through, why I'd been so eager to assume one death had anything to do with the others. Why had I so aggressively forced a clean narrative onto a simple series of unfortunate events? If I'd never come across the body of Hannan, if Thomas and I had had better luck, or a better relationship, would it have been so hard to see the Headmaster's death as not a murder at all but the desperate act of a man who'd simply had enough? Maybe he'd been miserable for months. Years. Maybe he was a man predisposed to misery. I hadn't known him to make a joke. I couldn't remember ever having seen a genuine smile on his face, nothing more than a grin. It followed that his wife might have known this all along, and might have seen it all coming. Murder seemed suddenly so far from probable, especially at the hands of a pack of boys, however malicious. His veins had been opened. His body left to be discovered in his office. It might have been his final gift to her, to have dispatched himself on campus rather than in the home they shared. Maybe even a practical decision, made with her in mind, or with her blessing. With his body in the office, far from their shared home, she could avoid the grisly scene altogether, and call in the state to clean it up.

I watched her face for any sign of what she knew and did not know. Of what she'd expected, or maybe seen and heard. She was peaceful. Simply peaceful. Comfortable with me, as if we were old friends. Here, now, she was without fear or anxiety. An enviable state. More than free, she wore the expression of those who have somehow glimpsed the depths of their experience, who have already toured the hell that they will one day occupy and long ago taken the necessary steps to prepare themselves to enjoy whatever time remained. I shook my head at how foolish I'd been. I'd known little more than fear and worry until now, even in my calmer moments. They had been my guiding lights. But here, by the fire, was something else.

I walked over to her and placed my hand on hers.

"Thank you, dear," she said, opening her eyes for only a moment.

I stood with her, and we did not speak for some time. She might have been sleeping.

This is what unity looked like, I decided. Not a swarm, but two peaceful bodies, quiet and still, before a warming fire. I longed for it, knowing full well this was something I might never find again outside of this moment, which I had to admit I'd stolen for myself while an old woman slept. I was a boy cast aside by society. More than cast aside, I was a boy society had never elected to touch. A boy without roots, without family. A boy in a sea of boys abandoned to be boys. What, after our time here was done, would I really have to offer?

"You look so serious, Ashley," she said. She'd been watching me wipe my cheeks and stare at the fire. "Everything is of such dire importance with you, from one moment to the next. I can't understand how you make it through the day without collapsing."

"I'm sorry," I said, setting my other hand with the first one. I crouched before her like a knight. "But my name isn't Ashley."

"Oh?" she said, smiling, though tight-lipped. "What would you like me to call you?"

I thought on it and found no word. I was myself. The boy I had always been. But no specific title found its way into my thoughts or onto my tongue. Just images of myself in the Headmaster's office, in the dormitory, bound and gagged, kicking toward the edge of the lake.

"Klot," I said, as it was all I could think to say.

She set her other hand to the top of my head.

THE JOB OF THE WASP

"I think it's too nasty," she said. "May I call you Ashley until we've come up with something better?"

It was very cold then, as if someone had opened a window and let in the night. I let her rub the top of my head as I wondered. My worry was back, but I didn't know why.

"Why Ashley?" I said.

"It's easier for me," she said, "to call you by the name I've known for you."

I struggled to understand what she meant but held my tongue. With every word we spoke, the peace I'd felt in our moment by the fire seemed further away, and I wanted only to sustain it for as long as I could.

"My memory isn't what it once was," she said, "as you know. Toward the end there is a limit to how much you can handle at once."

I was listening, but the cold had grown more severe. I checked to confirm that the fire had not gone out and saw it was roughly the same size as it had been when I'd come in. There was no open window I could see, and besides, who would have opened it?

"Ashley is fine, then," I said, taking away my hands to rub my arms. "May I put on another log?"

"Of course, Ashley," she said.

The firewood was stacked by the hearth, and I set two logs at cross angles on the fire. It wrapped around them in an instant, scorching the moss on the bark. I sat back in the Headmaster's chair with a shiver, happy to see the fire growing and that I had the Headmaster's wife's full attention. It felt like a position of some significance, to have her watching me. There was confidence in her expression that looked almost like friendly recognition. Or maybe it was peace. I honestly hadn't known either well enough to hazard a guess, but that she might still be feeling what I'd failed to hold on to for more than a moment seemed understandable, given the discrepancies in our respective understanding of the situation at hand. Even so, I thought of the metal vase ringing out against the stone porch. The fire, and how easily the image had come to me before of these chairs and of this room. Of the enormous green shawl.

"Ma'am," I said, matching her gaze, "why do you think you know who I am?"

She shrugged. "It's one of the first things that goes," she said, sitting back in her chair. "Short-term memory. There's nothing on which the new experiences can hang. Older memories linger, at least for a while. But they fade too, like the light of a candle, as the circles we walk grow smaller and smaller."

If I'd been cultivating poetic impulses before, it seemed the Headmaster's wife had entertained the spirit for some time.

"Ashley," she said. "About your bad news." She had a cigarette in her hand that I did not remember her lighting. But it was blocking the smell of the pumpkin, so I was pleased by its sudden introduction. "Do you mind if I make a guess?"

It was in bad taste to let her try, but she spoke with such confidence that it was not unlike being placed under a spell. I knew the likelihood of her guessing correctly was slim to none, but it is a problem with most humans that they seek to draw you into their understanding of the world and force a fit, assuming your experiences and intentions must be similar to their own, and that they understand you simply because they too have lived a life. I'm not blameless in this regard, but at least I've been able to perceive it as a shortcoming, rather than a triumph of perception. If this was confidence, if this was peace, if she truly did not have a care in the world, maybe it was only because, either by choice or the steady deterioration of her body with age, she had worn down the edges of her life so that they fit neatly within a framework of her own creation, beyond which she could no longer see any distinction. It wasn't so far from what Fry had been attempting, though perhaps with more malicious designs, in the dining hall. And it wasn't so far from what I'd been doing either, in my earlier efforts to explain the corpses piling up at my feet. It was understandable, maybe even unavoidable. But that didn't make it right.

Still, now that I'd seen some similarity between us, now that I understood we were of a kind, I was admittedly struck with a sick curiosity to hear what she might say. What she might imagine my bad news was, and how she had come to her particular conclusion.

"I don't mind," I said. Then I added, "Although it is truly bad news, and I don't wish to make light of it."

"Ms. Klein is dead," she said, tapping her cigarette while watching for my reaction.

I stayed as calm as I could, but I felt a sinister presence in the room. Something that might have been there all along, but was only just beginning to reveal itself.

She stayed focused on me as I registered the shift, and I could have sworn I saw a grin creep across her face before she broke it to ask, "Am I right?"

Instinctively, I listened for the thunder. But none came. Even the storm had left me.

"How did you know about Ms. Klein?" I said.

She smiled again, opening her mouth this time to reveal with grim pleasure the rotten landscape of her gums. They held only four front teeth, and the rest was a fleshy mess. A softly lit wound. The smell in the room worsened.

"I shouldn't enjoy being right about it," she said. "But there is something satisfying in a well-executed guess, regardless of the circumstances."

I'd heard of medical practices in which the teeth were removed due to a belief that insanity breeds in the bacteria born along the gum line, entering our nervous systems through the roots. It had only been a story before, nothing more, but here now sat the Headmaster's wife, grinning at me like an eel.

It was with great sadness and disappointment that I finally began to understand her confidence for what it was. Her air of detachment. It wasn't peace at all, but another piece of the puzzle, as it wasn't the Headmaster who was mad, nor any of the boys in his charge: It was his wife. It made sense now, that, though she lived just down the hill, we never saw her. She'd been locked away at the foot of our campus by the Headmaster, her husband, who, it stood to reason, would have done so out of fear for what she was capable of.

I could see now a scenario wherein the Headmaster's wife had grown tired of her dank prison, which smelled horrifically of pumpkin, and had executed an escape. With her newfound freedom she might have wandered the campus, its dark corridors and hidden areas, where she might have discovered Ms. Klein and the Headmaster—perhaps in the middle of their treacherous act, or by way of some hardly hidden piece of evidence, such as the drawings—in either case now faced with the reality of her husband, for more years than I had life, carrying on with his employee behind her back. If the Headmaster's wife had done and seen all that, might she have been mad enough to murder Ms. Klein and bury her body in the garden? Certainly the tilled earth would have made the work of digging a grave that much easier, and she was an older woman, and possibly grateful for the reprieve. It fit with the idea that I'd discovered the corpse by chance, bad timing on the Headmaster's part, who was dealing with the problem of too many boys and not enough work to go around, perhaps, and who had decided, just as summer began, that the solution was to turn back to the garden, thereby restoring to us the small pleasures it had once provided. In simpler times. It was a kindness of which I'd once assumed him incapable, but its impact lingered long after his death—though perhaps not in the way he might have hoped.

Thomas's death, then, was nothing but the unfortunate result of a bad situation gone worse. If I could have controlled my anger and my need to take the lead, Thomas might still be around to speak to our discovery and my innocence. But then, what of Hannan? Had he seen me unearth the corpse and murder Thomas, then dispose of the bodies in the lake? If Hannan had been watching me, he would have known I was innocent of the murder of Ms. Klein, and that Thomas's death was purely an accident. A terrible accident, yes, but not a malicious act. Hannan might even have been about to approach me when he was seized from behind by the Headmaster's wife, who could easily have been watching him watch me all along. No doubt, if she had escaped once she could do it again, and where there is an unresolved crime, I've been told, the nervous criminal often circles back to ensure his or her safety. Obsessively, it's said, will the criminal return, so it seemed entirely within the realm of possibility that the Headmaster's wife had been circling that same spot at the very moment when I arrived with Thomas, and had seen too that Hannan was making his way down, and had gone into hiding upon our discovery of Ms. Klein's corpse, remaining there through the consequent but accidental murder of Thomas. The Headmaster's wife would have watched Hannan as he watched me dispose of the bodies and, knowing that Hannan was my only resource for making a believable case for my innocence, as he was the only one left who might be willing to testify that what I was saying was in fact true, that the shadows of guilt in which I'd cast my alibi by disposing of the bodies were in fact only an illusion and that disposing of them had been an act of panic and fear, not a confirmation of malicious intent, she would have been able to defend to herself one more murder to help resolve these unexpected developments, and might then have taken Hannan into her home, poisoned him (which would explain the absence of wounds), and set him in my closet to further darken my good name and render questionable any claims I made toward innocence.

I saw again, in the ghastly smile this madwoman wore as she watched me struggle to understand what she'd presented, the tragedy of our shared situation on this earth: that most truths are inconceivable to us, as they sit just beyond the limits of our ability to comprehend them. I could never have guessed what I would find in this house, not without visiting it, which I'd only done because I'd become invested in an idea that was wholly false. It was only through this potentially fatal error that I'd come to understand what was right and what might have saved me. If I'd been able to perceive the truth of the matter on my own, as I'd been trying to do for so long now, I might have stayed out of harm's way. And yet, it was only in harm's way that I could see it for what it was.

If I was in danger, I was not lost. The night was far from over, and the decisions I would make in the coming moments would determine which of us actually controlled the fate of the other, as well as of the boys now gathered at the top of the hill. Something would have to be done, here and now, but what it was I did not yet know. I watched her, and I waited for the plan to present itself.

"In a private moment between us," she said, "Ms. Klein communicated a belief that committing such an act might improve our situation at the facility, and through my many years on this earth I've learned that where there is that particular will, there is always and without fail a way."

"You're saying she took her own life?" I said.

"Do you doubt it?" she said flatly, as a liar might.

The fire snapped a coal onto the carpet, and the Headmaster's wife just let it burn.

"But why would she do that?" I said, feeling my confidence return in her absence of sense.

Hidden away, she might have once been a powerful force, but now, in the full light of the fire, I saw her madness as a weakness I could exploit. If I was careful, if I could come to understand the unique contours of her broken rationality, there was hope.

"She loved you boys," she said. "She was devoted to you."

The ember smoked and faded, as the ash had, and I

realized I could not recall the particulars of Ms. Klein's face. Only her gnarled fingers in the dirt, the weight of her body in the wheelbarrow.

"She wanted to be with you," she said. "She wanted it more than anything her life in the village had to offer. You have to understand, she wasn't a woman of means or talent. She wasn't a person people gravitated toward, and she didn't particularly like them anyway. As a result, she had been alone for many years. When we took her in, we had no idea how suddenly and completely she would come to love you boys, or how quickly her work would become the focus of her life."

"Then how devastating for us that she's gone," I said.

"Ashley," said the Headmaster's wife. She leaned in, catching the light of the fire in her grotesque cavern of a mouth. "You haven't stopped shivering. Can I fix you something warm to drink?"

"We were already stretched to the limit with boys like you when the state started sending us sick ones," said the Headmaster's wife. "My husband went into town each year to present our case to the state," she said, "to tell them how thinly stretched our resources were. It didn't matter to them, of course. Their facilities were as jammed as ours, and boys were already being turned away, made to sleep without beds, made to last days without food."

The tea she'd brought me was like lake water—metallic, vaguely vegetal—but it was warm, and so soothing that I found myself quickly feeling comfortable in a way I had not since I'd held her hand by the fire. With each sip, I felt more

like myself. Less anxious. Less afraid. More capable of understanding her, and how I might safely be able to remove myself
from this unexpected situation, without causing alarm, in order to alert the other boys.

"Crowded as we were, we knew we could offer the sick
boys a decent enough end," she said, "and thereby be the better
of two bad options. The decision to cut Ms. Klein wasn't an
easy one. Our numbers grew with each semester, and the situation became so dire, we could no longer pay her or feed her
or house her without eating into the resources we needed for
the boys in our care. The state was no longer sending only sick
boys, but challenging boys, boys who needed special attention.
'Bad apples,' they called them. Rotten souls who would fare
better in a controlled environment. What were we to do? Turn
them away? Send them back to a society that had already once
pushed them out? We did what we could. We made the decision to release Ms. Klein. She was old enough to have another
life and young enough to have some fun with it, if she were so
inclined, or to find another school and another set of boys to
love and educate and comfort."

It was either the tea or the fresh logs I'd added to the fire,
but I was no longer shivering. My muscles had relaxed into the
chair, and I could feel that where I'd once held fear, I now held
nothing. My body was like a cushion for the brain that held it
in place, and it was a pleasant enough feeling, after all I'd been
through. I listened, watching her and sipping my tea. No doubt
I was still in danger, but my awareness of it was very clean, un-
compromised by my anxieties, which I had abandoned to the
floor of her home, like the ember and the ash.

"But the decision didn't stick," said the Headmaster's wife, rocking ever so slightly now in her chair. "Ms. Klein kept coming back to us, the poor thing. With such passion and consistency that I couldn't help wondering if she'd lost her sense along the way. There is a madness in loyalty, in that kind of devotion. You become blind to the possibilities of life, sacrificing the present, and the future, to the past."

"I don't agree," I said, but it came out almost like a yawn. I wanted to say that loyalty was something I imagined could grant an otherwise inconsequential life meaning, and that devotion to others kept some from living exclusively for themselves. But the moment I paused to consider them, my thoughts seemed suddenly too far from me to collect.

"Neither did Ms. Klein," she said. "Ms. Klein had a theory, as I'm sure you do, Ashley, and a plan. We'd known of the stories for some time, and we saw it as perfectly natural for children in a facility such as ours to imagine something so grandiose as a life that could be lived in its halls after death, particularly when the sick boys began to go. Who could blame them? But when Ms. Klein proposed to us her plan to return to the facility after her own self-inflicted death, we were at a loss for what to do. We'd clearly allowed things to get out of hand. We knew the matter would have to be dealt with, and in a way that mitigated harm. We could have had her committed, but given that the joys she'd found in this life were so limited, it seemed unduly cruel to lock her away. And what right did we really have to interfere? After all, it's possible this was something she'd been working up the nerve to do even before we knew her. It's possible she'd had the plan for years but had only just found a socially acceptable justification to see it through.

"I have no love for suicides," she said. "I find the self-absorption involved exhausting. But if she was doing it for you boys, she might have reasoned, what was self-absorbed about that? Dead, as she explained it to us, she would require no food, no rest, no comforts. And, conveniently, she would have no memory of her departure. She could haunt our halls for as long as they held, feeling as alive as ever and helping you all without taxing our resources. Madness, we were certain of it. But a notion such as hers is a lock not easily picked."

It seemed to comfort her, ascribing to Ms. Klein the very diagnosis that had undoubtedly cast a shadow over her own life. But in her tale of our teacher's demise, the Headmaster's wife had clarified little more for me than her own insanity. The more she spoke, the better I understood that there was no ghost in our facility. No ghost, and no ghosts. Ms. Klein was nothing other than a corpse tied to a rock in a lake, and her murderer was a red mess in a green shawl, jamming together whatever sketches of reality still existed in her virtually tooth-less skull. By now my body was so relaxed, either from the tea or from simple exhaustion, I was hardly more than a nub in her dead husband's chair. But I was not without my critical faculties. I needed only to keep her talking, and I would be safe. There would be an opportunity for escape soon enough. My body would return to me eventually, or the morning would overwhelm us, shedding new light on the proceedings and maybe even bringing a few of the other boys down the hill to come to my aid.

"Even when her plan worked," said the Headmaster's wife, "it brought us no relief to see her wandering the halls, day after day, clueless to the nature of her predicament."

She almost laughed. I could hear the lift in her voice as she spoke.

"You can't imagine," she said, "what it was like for her to come up to us while we were walking the grounds, day after day, and forfeit her salary, over and over again. Imagine the tragedy of it happening once. Now imagine that tragedy occurring every few days or so, even multiple times in one day, each time with renewed zeal and sincerity. Madame and Mister, she would call us, though we were anything but noble or decent. 'Madame and Mister, for the sake of the children.' It was clear to both of us that we were complicit in something terrible, that exploiting a lost soul was a damnable offense, even if it was in the interest of the school and, in truth, that very soul's dying wish. She'd turned hers into an eternity of suffering for the facility. And on top of that, you boys kept digging her up. It was all simply too much for us to take."

I was much drowsier than I'd realized. I couldn't even find it in my neck to shake my head. I could only bring my chin to my shoulder and watch the floor. When I blinked, my eyelids held together for several seconds before I could open them again, and my teacup fell to the carpet, where it split.

"But seeing Ms. Klein again," she said, "after what she'd done, it brought our unexplained occurrences here sharply into focus. The grisly mishaps, piling up over the years, seemed suddenly too coincidental to be overlooked. You boys always had stories, but they were only that: the stories of children. So we did some reading. And we tried to arm ourselves against the nightmares to come."

I brought my head back to center, where I felt my jaw fall open and hang. The depths of her madness, and its obvious influence on the inhabitants of our facility, were, in their own distorted way, impressive. What evils had she provoked by spreading these ideas, by allowing her insanity to infect the isolated boys in her care? Had she twisted them so completely as to turn them against one another, or had they always had those murderous impulses and she'd merely provided an outlet? I knew I had to be careful now. She was undoubtedly trying to influence me, as she had been so successful in doing with the other boys, whose faces I could not recall, exhausted and limp as I was in the chair. I could listen, I could learn, but I could not let her distort what I knew to be true. These weren't explanations but ghoulish obscenities meant to obscure all she had done. I held on to that thought as well as I could, understanding it would be my only salvation as the night grew longer.

"Why do you suppose a ghost haunts?" she said, watching me struggle with my neck.

I had an answer, but I could not manage it.

"They have lost their ability to connect to a world that no longer belongs to them," she said. "Memories fade to the point where they can't remember why they've made a particular choice, or that a choice was made at all, at least not for very long. A ghost will circle whatever feels familiar, or whatever starts to feel familiar after a period of aimless wandering. They will circle and circle until the possibility of the afterlife presents itself again, or the light of the candle finally burns out, and they are fully lost. A spirit turning in the yard without anything behind the act that could even resemble a conscious mind. It's a pitiable state, whatever gruesome affairs it may yield, but not something to be afraid of, Ashley.

Not here. Not with me." She smiled kindly as my eyes began to water.

How had she so effectively gotten through to the others? We were young, it's true, but surely not all so foolish as to buy into the ravings of a lunatic woman missing most of her teeth. What was the quality of this facility that led each of its inhabitants to readily abandon the knowns of our corporeal existence in favor of supernatural flights of fancy? Why did they all need to believe so desperately in something more?

Had I seen things I couldn't explain? Yes. Was there something to all of this that I couldn't hope to understand given the limited tools at my disposal? Perhaps. But ghosts? It seemed the most obvious expression of the limitations of human imagination to propose an experience beyond our lived one that simply mirrored what we've already been through in vaguely distorted ways. The sheer lack of ingenuity seemed evidence enough of the unlikelihood of her proposition, and yet no one in my cohort had been able to see through it? I would have laughed if I wasn't so tired. If I didn't feel drained beyond the point of even cracking my jaw back into place or reopening my mouth to explain that I hadn't come down to discuss Ms. Klein at all, in fact, or her supposed ghost, or that her death felt like a thing so far in the past to me that it seemed hardly worth mentioning, especially in light of all that had happened since. Ms. Klein was gone, and to where I knew precisely, as I'd weighted her down and left her there myself.

I watched the Headmaster's wife, wondering if she might understand some of this in the dull look I now gave her. And I will say that there was something like a fire, fueled by what might have been fear or righteousness, that seemed to light in her eyes then, as if she had somehow heard everything I had to say and understood its implications.

"I can see you have doubts," she said. "But I would encourage you to take me at my word. Skepticism is often no more than the sound of an unenlightened listener, clumsily winding his watch."

"Your husband," I slurred, "is dead."

I don't know where I found the energy, or how the words took shape in the slack of my jaw, but they fell from me nonetheless and met her only a few feet away.

Her face was still, though the air in the room had changed once more. I felt a release as my original mission, stalled as it had been by her attempts to draw me elsewhere, came to its intended conclusion. I felt that the Headmaster's chair could fold around me, and that I might sleep for an eternity in the stink of its embrace. I saw in her face the truth of her life as she'd known it fading so that reality might take its place. Here was something she hadn't been able to guess, and something for which her madness, however inventive it was, had not accounted.

"Henry," she said, gathering herself near the edge of her chair. "I should have known. That you're here again, and he is not, was enough to tell me something was wrong." She set her teacup on the table at her side. "You've come to confess," she said.

"No," I might have said, though I sat there frozen instead, thinking the word as hard as I could.

"Thank you," she said, with a sigh of what sounded like genuine relief. It was almost touching. "I've never relished this position," she said, "which is why I keep to myself and out of the way this time of year. But I knew upon your arrival here to-night, Ashley, that the core of our facility's concerns remained unresolved."

What had I missed? Where had her cigarette gone? Maybe she'd left it in the kitchen when she'd gone to fetch the tea. I imagined myself speaking but made no sound. I only watched her, blankly, as her tears escaped.

"How did you do it, Ashley?" she said. She tapped two fingers to the wrist of her opposite arm. "Did you open his veins?" she said.

I blinked twice for no. I looked to my hands, which sat like strangers on the armrests of the Headmaster's chair. I thought to move them, and when I couldn't, I realized I was not tired at all. I was not exhausted by the day, but awake and alert. Ready to act. My mind simply had no power over its body.

I'd never experienced anything like it before, this strange paralysis that seemed to me, more than anything, mental. As if I was thinking about the movements I wanted to make in the wrong way. They seemed within my reach; I could imagine them happening. And yet, nothing did.

"Ashley," she said, shaking her head. "How could you?"

"I've done nothing," I would have said. "Now please help me up." But instead of saying any of it, I realized that I had started to drool, or felt that I had. Humiliated, on the verge of hopelessness, the drawings returned to me as evidence of more than just an ongoing affair between the Headmaster and Ms. Klein. If his wife hadn't murdered him, then he'd taken his own life, and he'd surrounded himself with images of the woman he loved before doing so. He had chosen to die among them, rather than at home with this creature, who was possibly a murderer twice over and who would, in that case, be more than ready to add to that number, should anyone challenge her or stand in her way. Whoever had taken Ms. Klein's life, the Headmaster had made his final effort to return to her in the only way he'd imagined possible. If what the Headmaster's wife had said of Ms. Klein's plan was true, he'd possibly taken up that same delusion, out of sheer desperation, believing that in doing as he had done he would be granted an eternity alongside the object of his affection: a potentially sane woman, and one with her set of teeth still intact. It made tragic sense in a way that left me undone, and I was again impressed with my ability to empathize in the most difficult of times.

"I've always had a bad feeling about you," said the Headmaster's wife. "Since the day you arrived. Overweight, disinterested, unkind. I saw nothing worthy of any investment on my part, but Henry insisted you could be reached. He was always too generous with children."

She let a tear fall, but it was not sadness I saw in her expression. It was anger.

I should have seen it coming, but I realized then that I had always been optimistic to a fault. Instead of helping her, I had allowed myself to become the locus of all the feelings I'd unleashed in her upon delivering the news of her husband's demise. The more aware she was of all she had not known and could not know, the angrier she became, and, with the precision of a mousetrap, her broken mind had turned against the first defenseless creature to have wandered her way.

"How many is that?" she said. "One for now? Or two? Or are there others hidden in cupboards and dumbwaiters and piles of leaves around the campus? And, tell me, was I overly generous in assuming you'd let Ms. Klein take care of herself?"

With my body now frozen to the chair, my mind sped on, imagining all that was about to happen and the odds I had of saving myself. I struggled to reconcile the images I held in my thoughts of me getting up, of me running, of me scrambling up the hill as the Headmaster's wife bolted after, with the reality that I was doing none of those things. Something had changed inside of me. Something was different in the relationship of my mind to its body, as if a link between the two had been severed. But I was thinking as clearly as I ever had. I felt as though something had crawled into me and nestled in whatever part of my brain might have activated my strength, leaving me captive here in a rotten house just out of view of the lake. I thought of the corpses I'd left there, bound together for eternity. What if I'd been wrong? What if there was still something inside Thomas, something inside Ms. Klein, pulsing away against the fate I'd forced upon them? It seemed no accident to me that the tea had tasted of lake water. If the Headmaster's wife had truly turned against me, if she had put something in the drink that might have reduced my physical prowess in order to make me a more manageable target for her devastation, if she had put this all in motion with the only gift I'd accepted that evening, my body also understood this was a punishment come full circle. It had given me a taste, in that moment, of what I'd done to the poor souls of Thomas and Ms. Klein.

If it was poison, if I had in fact been paralyzed, I marveled at the ability of the Headmaster's wife to have seen this coming. How had she been so prepared? And I realized that those who've done the most wrong will likely always exceed the rest of us in their ability to imagine and account for the worst. Or, more simply, she was insane. She was a murderer. And this was nothing more than what they did.

She was moving now, out of her seat, and I knew the time had come to deliver my defense. I could speak, at least some, I'd proven that, but my arms and legs were unresponsive. My head had been able to loll from one shoulder to the other, but not smoothly and only with great effort. She made her way to the mantel, smiling with that hollow, open mouth again, as if the expression had been scooped from the flesh of her face. I danced for her, lolling spasmodically, but couldn't draw her attention from a picture frame she'd taken from the shelf above the fire. The frame was draped with a small black curtain, obscuring whatever image was behind its glass. She lifted that curtain, and her smile faded, replaced with something like sadness, or anger, or disgust, a feeling that made her sigh, quickly, before transforming her expression into one of firm resolve. It had to have been a photo of the Headmaster, but at what stage in his life, I could only guess. Maybe it was a photo of him as a boy.

How I managed to feel brokenhearted in that moment of mounting terror, I can't say. I only know that I watched the Headmaster's wife and felt a mix of things more productive than fear. I felt sadness and rage at what she'd done, at what she'd been able to accomplish and obscure, while I'd blindly crept into her grasp like an ant into a bowl of water. I felt absurdly confident too, and, in a truly pathetic moment, believed my rage would bring me out of the chair and over to her, where I could knock the picture from her hands and pin her to the ground, taking control of the situation and rescuing the others from what I was increasingly sure would be a gruesome fate. This was more than a punishment delivered upon me for the sins I'd committed, and more than the final stage of an elaborate and macabre cover-up for two jealous murders of passion. This was a woman who had been enjoying herself.

With that, the grim utility of our facility settled in. As the bodies piled up, boy after boy would continue to arrive. There would never be a shortage of boys. Sick boys, disturbed boys, boys with nowhere else to turn, like myself and poor Hannan. If she'd been eager to cast the blame and be done with it, she would have had me long ago. Instead, she was carrying on with me here, settling into another sadistic smile as she placed the picture back on the mantel, moved toward the kitchen, and vanished through the French doors, returning, after only a moment, with a butcher's knife I recognized immediately as one from the dining hall set.

"I was happy to hope the boys had resolved the matter last year," she said. "I won't go so far as to say I felt relief, but I did feel that a weight had been lifted."

The knife was too large for her withered hands, and it was laughable to think any real harm could come from such an ill-suited instrument.

"I've done nothing," I thought, "no harm to anyone," which wasn't exactly true but was closer to the truth than what she seemed to be thinking. I felt the drool at my lip, tugging the flesh ever so slightly as it ran from the edge of my mouth when I tried to speak.

"Of course, it's not the first time they were wrong," she said. "There's often more to these things than can be responsibly considered before the time to act has come and gone. Maybe it was nothing more than cowardice on my part, but I could have sworn they'd had it right."

She approached, and I sat like a fish beaten against the bottom of a boat, working the hinge of my jaw at the smallest detectable angle.

"Do you know what else a ghost does?" she said. She brought the blade close in order to rub my lips and chin with the sleeve of her shawl. "Other than forget? Other than circle?"

I could smell on her the rot I'd noticed upon entering. I prayed back the impulse to vomit, afraid I would choke.

"They trace the meaningful gestures they made in life," she said. "Or those they found meaningful. Like a recurring dream, you find yourself there, again and again, feeling the same, even if each time it's a little different."

A dream, I thought. Maybe. Sure. Was it so crazy to think I might have been responding to feelings of isolation, fear, loneliness, by playing out these dark scenarios and missteps in my sleep? It wasn't hard to picture myself curled up on my thin mattress all this time, the voices of my tormentors traveling through the window near my desk. After all, could I remember the last time I'd actually slept through the night? I'd had dreams like this before, a body unable to move as something inexplicably threatening approached. I remembered sliding through the mud instead of walking, a rigid mass holding me under the water like a palm, my trouser leg tearing, just as I'd feared it would. I couldn't get over how comical the enormous knife looked in her pale and fragile hands. I felt, if she were to raise it, it would tear through them like a web.

"I always thought you came here because you had some

mother figure you'd disappointed in life," she said, "and from whom you were seeking consolation. Maybe even resolution. I understand now that it might have been guilt of an entirely different nature. And though I despise you, I do hope you have found something you can take with you when you leave."

"I've never known my mother," I might have yelled, if I could have yelled. "There is no one in my life whose disappointment would matter to me at all," I might have shouted as I ran for the door.

"That's the tragedy of those things that mean the most to us in life," she said. "That from where you sit, Ashley, from where we will all sit one day, they're lost. Their influence may push us along, like a wind at our backs, but we can't know them for what they are, and neither can anyone else."

"I'm not Ashley," I said, surprised again to feel my lips and throat fall in line with one of the countless impulses rattling off in my brain. There was a trick to it, that much was clear, as I was able to manage to speak sometimes, but not others. That I'd been doing it wrong for the most part only meant that it was something I could master.

"No," she said to me. "You are a demon."

"I'm a boy," I thought. All I had ever been.

"I'll admit I'm ashamed it took me so long to see the truth," she said. "All these years you've been with us, and yet the cost of seeing you as you are was still so high."

I knew she was wrong. I'd only just arrived. I could remember it. I could see everything exactly as it had happened. At least for the most part.

"You're confused," she said. "I can see it in the way you're thinking. But don't be afraid. I can't hurt you. I can only show you what you are, and in that small way, perhaps, offer us both some relief."

The smell of her filled my nostrils like smoke. That smell like a pumpkin on a porch in the sun. I gagged but nothing came up, and when I inhaled, it curled deeper into my lungs.

"Confession or no, you are dead and doing harm," she said, "and I will prove it to you. I only hope you'll take the opportunity to leave us before you hurt more of those who wanted nothing but to help you along the way."

Fear did not leave me in this, the most difficult moment of my life. Nor did it grip my mind so completely as to wipe out every other possible feeling, forcing me to focus on it exclusively. Instead, I expanded. I became aware of new emotional textures, new contours of thought, as if a switch had been flipped, and I was capable of holding more ideas at once than I had ever have imagined, more states of being, more contradictions and impossibilities, which is why I was struck, though not entirely surprised, to find myself feeling both deeply afraid, more frightened than I had ever felt before, and, at the same time and with undeniable severity, curious. On top of everything else, I simply wanted to know the truth. I'd managed to keep my wits over the course of our conversation, but I'd been no doubt seduced by the question of her madness, struggling to work out the degree to which she had invented the entire scenario and the degree to which she was describing the world as it actually was, myself as I actually was, and as I was—according to my nature as she described it—unable to see myself without someone else's guidance. And, if I were actually unable to see myself as I truly was without her guidance, if, in her absence, I was doomed to go on seeing less and less, doomed to wander this world without memory or purpose, was it true that it was a violent and unpredictable circle I would trace, or would it instead be the path of the curious, of those openly engaged with the mysteries of this world, as I would have imagined for myself, and in which case, I had to wonder, given the circumstances, would I forever be subjected to the machinations of life's most manipulative malcontents, as I had been so far? Mad as she may have been, she was perceptive. Perceptive as she was, she had her sights set on doing me harm.

Or—I briefly, optimistically allowed—this was all a test. An elaborate staging to get me to confess to all, or one of, my many crimes, or to an unknown crime I'd been suspected of since before I'd even come to an awareness of any suspicion directed my way. The idea that this was a dream, that this was all the product of an ill-at-ease mind, came to me again and provided some small comfort, like an opiate or a fist to the skull. I thought, and thought again. How easy it is to forget. How easy it is to doubt. How plainly did the realization arrive that I tended to doubt myself most in the moments when I should have been most confident, while being assured in the moments when, as I'd witnessed time and again that evening, I couldn't have been farther from the truth. How difficult it can be to coordinate thought and action. But how tragic the lives of those who never try. And, too, how bitterly fitting it was to realize that, after all I had seen and all the work I had done, all I had lived through and all I had thought, I was unable to move myself from the chair of my beloved Headmaster and return to the facility for orphaned boys, where the others had returned, and where a life of some unexpected kind might have been waiting, but was instead still sitting there before the

Headmaster's wife, the largest knife in her little hand, thinking to myself over and over again, *You are alive, you are alive, you are alive and it is something that you know,* only to have her draw the blade from my wrist to my elbow, opening my swollen veins to confirm it.

ACKNOWLEDGMENTS

Though the list of artists and artworks to which this novel is indebted would be a fat book in itself, I'd be remiss if I didn't credit and thank the following for the undeniable influence of their accomplishments:

Henry James's *The Sacred Fount* · Robert Walser · Patty Yumi Cottrell · Brian Evenson · Helen Oyeyemi · John Clare · Guillermo del Toro · Hernan Diaz's *In the Distance* · Anonymous · Fred Mustard Stewart's *The Mephisto Waltz* · Barbara Comyns · Bruno Schulz · Marie NDiaye · Andrei Tarkovsky · Haley Joel Osment · Victor LaValle · Jeremy Davies · Jesse Ball · Wallace Stevens · Andi Winnette.

Thanks to Yuka Igarashi, Wah-Ming Chang, and everyone at Soft Skull/Catapult/Counterpoint, who worked so hard to bring this book into the world. And to Jonathan Lee, who had a colleague take a look.

Thanks to Charlotte Sheedy, my agent, mentor, and friend, who saw this book for what it wanted to be. Thanks for fighting for it, and for standing by my side since the day we met.

ACKNOWLEDGMENTS

To the early readers of the mess, especially Daniel Levin Becker, who will one day write the theatrical adaptation: thank you.

And to bug, as always, for everything.